Adventures of a Countryside Boy

Dr. Thomas T Thomas

Copyright © 2022 Dr. Thomas T Thomas
All rights reserved.
No part of this book may be produced or stored in a retrieval system or transmitted in any form by any means, electronic, photocopying, recording, or otherwise, without express written permission of the publisher.

The characters and events portrayed in this book are fictitious. Any similarity to real persons, living or dead, is coincidental and not intended by the author.

Cover design by Ranjit Jose
ranjitjos@gmail.com

DEDICATION

This book is dedicated to my wife

Jessy

(Dr. Annie George)

ACKNOWLEDGMENTS

I acknowledge with extreme gratitude

My family for the support and encouragement

Ms. Molly Kurian, for suggesting an apt title,

Ms. Anu T. Thomas and **Ms. Roina Annie Koshy**, for help in editing the book,

Mr. Som Bathla and **Ms. Sweta Samota**, my mentors,

Mr. Ranjit Jose for the cover design,

Mr. Aju A. Varghese for formatting the book contents, and

All my friends and former classmates for their support and encouragement.

CONTENTS

1. Two Different Worlds 7
2. Paradise on Earth 11
3. Bombay (Now Mumbai) 16
4. School in Mumbai 21
5. Book Uncle 25
6. Entertainment in Bombay 28
7. Tragedy 32
8. Valiammachi 37
9. Dr. Kampu 43
10. Countryside School 48
11. A Ghostly Encounter 54
12. Satisfaction for Men of Action 59
13. Sir Isaac Newton and David Sir 64
14. A Costly Trip Home 69
15. 'Born Again' 74
16. Emergency 78
17. Vellore Medical College 82
18. Unborn Again! 88
19. A Mysterious Light from the Grave 93
20. College Elections During Emergency 97
21. A Meek Revolutionary 101
22. The End of Emergency 106
23. A Piece of Fried Banana 112
24. Zoology Student 117
25. A Student Politician 121
26. Ticketless Travel 127
27. Study Tour 131

28. Final Exam	135
29. Kerala to Tamilnadu	140
30. The Virgin Princess	146
31. Heroes, Ourselves	150
32. Triumphant Return	157
33. Fate in the Balance	160
34. The Celebration	165
35. A Medical Student!	168
Epilogue	172

1. Two Different Worlds

"What is the Hindi word for fish?" Leelamma Teacher, our Hindi tutor, threw the challenge in our class. She was a passionate teacher in her forties and loved by all, given that she rarely wielded the cane.

I know that one! I have even used the word several times while going to the local fish market in Bombay. My hand shot up.

"Yes?" Leelamma Teacher smiled and prompted me.

"Machi!" I was confident and responded loudly, but the entire class burst out laughing.

"What! What did you say?" The smile had gone from the teacher's face, and an angry scowl took its place. She trembled in anger as she raised the cane, poised to strike at me.

"Machi," I repeated, this time much softer and not very sure.

Whack! I felt the searing pain on my left arm as she brought the rod down on me with all her might. I looked up, perplexed and frightened. Her eyes were blazing hot and wet with tears. The laughter in the class died down abruptly.

Leelamma Teacher pulled me by the collar to the front of the class and kept beating me from top to bottom, left and right. She then dragged me to the Staff Room straight to my mother, a teacher in the same school.

"He called me 'Machi' in front of the entire class!" Leelamma Teacher sobbed loudly as she complained to my mother, who looked up from the examination papers she was checking and opened her mouth wide in surprise.

I saw my mother's eyes widen as she looked at me, and said. "I am sure he wouldn't do anything like that."

"She asked me the Hindi word for fish and started beating me as soon as I answered," I told her in between sobs, and my mother's face lit up with understanding.

"Teacher, that is what they say for fish in Bombay. Everyone in the market says 'Machi' for fish. I know the proper Hindi word is 'Machili,' but 'Machi' is a Marathi slang used there."

Leelamma teacher looked at her and then at me, and enlightenment dawned on her. She broke into tears and grabbed me again- this time, in a tight hug. "Sorry," she mumbled into my ear. I started crying too, more from the sharp pains over my body.

I learned later that 'Machi' was a colloquial word (a mean one too) in Malayalam to denote a barren woman, and Leelamma Teacher was indeed childless. She was aware of the children using this word as a nickname behind her back- no wonder she was so furious when someone called her so to her face.

I had joined midway in class five at this school in Kerala, returning from Bombay. Despite such hiccups, I felt liberated from the school from where I had come.

We- myself and my younger brother had come back for good with my mother, leaving my father behind until he completed his stint there. He was a Vicar of our church in Bombay and had a minimum tenure of three years at one place. He felt this best for us- especially for my mother. A change of circumstances might ease her grief over the death of Leelamol, my two-year-old sister, who was buried there. My brother was too young to fathom the loss, and my father was stoic and accepting of the tragedy. Whenever I thought about Leelamol, I felt a dull heaviness in my chest, but my mother could never get over the pain, often given to crying spells many times throughout the day.

This school was a far cry from the stifling atmosphere of the school in Bombay and the suffocating congestion of the city. The grip of the tie around my neck and the shoes on my feet added to the choked feeling. *Why should we emulate this western dress in our hot and humid climate?*

No one wore shoes here, and most students didn't even wear chappals. A necktie was unthinkable, and I believe most students here wouldn't even have seen one.

We stayed with my maternal grandparents in Thiruvalla, an old and docile town in central Kerala. Life was dull compared to my father's family house thirty-five kilometers away, in a village called Mallassery.

Memories of my first visit there soon after returning from Bombay created a craving to go there as often as possible. The two weeks I spent there were akin to my concept of life in Paradise.

I had gone to visit Valiyammachi, our grandma, and my cousins. It was my first solo long-distance trip since my return. Carrying a bag with some clothes and a toothbrush, I traveled by bus as far as it would take me and walked the remaining five kilometers to reach our house by evening to an enthusiastic welcome.

2. Paradise on Earth

"Wait for me!" I cried out loud, but nobody seemed to notice. They hurried across the paddy field on the narrow ledge dividing the plots- five of them, three boys and two girls, all my cousins. I was the sixth, a fresher, having just returned from the metropolis. I had just turned ten, and we were all between seven and thirteen.

The strip was just about a foot wide, and the plot on my left was four feet below. I put my foot down on the precarious ridge. They had helped me down the slippery slope to the paddy field, but once on level ground, they urged me to follow them and scampered across in a single line. "Remove your chappals. You will slip with them on," someone shouted to me.

It was mid-June 1969, and the *Kaalavarsham*- the Southwest Monsoon, was in full swing. The rain had been unrelenting all day, as it had been throughout the night. By late afternoon, when the sky cleared, we lost no time rushing outdoors. It was a vast expanse of land, still kept undivided since my grandfather's death ten years ago, when I was born.

"Walk briskly," Kochettan urged. 'Kochettan' was a name I had made up for him, the youngest among my older cousin brothers. As I put my foot on the ledge again, I could feel the slimy earth underneath and stood there hesitating. "Put your back foot in front before you slip, and don't break the pace."

I followed their advice to the letter and went forward a few steps before I felt like losing my balance. Thinking it better to make a run for it, I dashed forward, but before I knew it, I was diving face down into the watery mud. I felt myself choking as the slime got into my eyes, ears, nose, and mouth. But then, my whole body braced for a violent cough, followed by an even more violent sneeze, and I could breathe again.

"What's this you've done? We came to help you, and you have sprayed mud all over us!" Kochettan looked at me accusingly. They all had come running back, seeing me fall.

"I can't see!" I cried as I looked at him, seeing only a muddy blur. I tried to rub my eyes clear, but it just got messier.

"Don't rub your eyes!" He shouted at me and told the others. "We must get him to the stream and wash him up."

A meandering stream ran on the other side of the paddy field, but I was not willing to get back on the ledge and walk toward it.

"Let's pull him to it," Kochettan said as he scrambled up the embankment and broke off a strong twig. He made me hold it at one end, and they took turns to grip the other end and pull me to the opposite bank through the mud.

It was a smooth enough ride, though I banged my shoulder several times on the sidewalls of the ledge that separated the higher plot. Once at the other side, they pulled me up to the bank, and we scrambled across to the narrow stream flowing parallel to the paddy field.

They laid me face down in the shallow water that flowed in a steady stream, which washed the mud off my face. After washing my hands, I splashed water onto my face and eyes. I could see again! The shiny pebbles on the floor of the stream shone brightly, but around where I lay, the water became muddy.

"You are carrying all the mud inside your clothes. Take them off!" Kochettan and my elder cousin, Sabuchettan, worked on me. Despite my protests, they began pulling out my shirt and briefs, leaving me stark naked in the water. The girls giggled.

I got the slime off me, washed my clothes in the clear flowing water, and got rid of all the mud. "Wait till it gets dried," Kochettan said, laying them out on the bank.

"At least let me wear my shorts!" I pleaded as I grabbed it and put it on. They all roared with laughter as if I had done something funny.

"Let's all take a bath," Sabuchettan suggested, "but this water is too shallow. We'll make a dam and raise the water level."

Kochumol, Kochettan's younger sister, ran back to the house to fetch a knife. Kochettan and Sabuchettan scurried up the high bank on the other side, where banana plants grew in a field. Several trees already harvested stood with the stem cut in the middle, the leaves with the stump of the harvested fruit slumped down to the ground. The boys got to work, cutting off the soft cylindrical stems into five to six-foot-long pieces.

"Don't stand there watching! Do something to help." Sabuchettan scolded me. "Carry these logs to the stream, and be careful! Don't let them get carried away in the flow."

I tried to lift one of the smaller logs onto my shoulder, but the weight was too much, and I fell with the log on top of me- more laughter. "Get the girls to help you," Kochettan said, laughing as he cut another long piece and stripped off the outer dried layers. He cut off the top with the leaves. "Don't forget to collect all the good leaves. Valiammachi will be glad to serve us dinner in them. It will save her the trouble of washing dishes."

Valiammachi was our grandma, who cooked tasty local dishes for us. All of us flocked here not only for the fun of the outdoors but also for the delicacies she cooked for us.

We stripped off the outer layers of a couple of delicate stems to take out the white, glistening, cylindrical core, which looked like a tube light. Valiammachi would make a tasty dish with this inner stem, shredding it into tiny pieces and cooking with shallots, green chilies, and coconut gratings.

Getting Kochumol to hold up one end of the log, I grabbed the other end, and we rushed to the stream. "Keep it leaning up against the side and collect the other ones," Kochettan instructed.

I lowered the log into the stream, but it slipped from my hands and was immediately swept away by the flow. I saw it getting caught by some tall grass in the water and rushed after it, but it cleverly dislodged itself and happily continued on its way downstream.

"Shit! You have lost a good one. Anyway, get the rest, and be careful not to lose any more. We are going down into the stream to make the dam."

Sabuchettan and Kochettan climbed down into the stream, carrying a log each on their shoulders. They cut the ends just long enough to place them across the stream jammed tight against the side walls. "Now, don't stand there just watching," Sabuchettan reminded me again. "Bring all the logs here."

I ran with the girls to fetch the rest of the logs. I would place them erect on the high land and push them into the stream with a warning shout. They stacked them up across the creek, and the water level rose. "Just one more to come!" I shouted as we rushed to fetch the last log.

"That will be enough." Jollyammamma, Sabuchettan's elder sister and the oldest among us, reminded me. "We have strict instructions that if we build a dam here, we should not make it higher than our chest level."

The last one was heavier, and we were huffing and puffing as we got it to the bank. Holding it erect on the high bank, I pushed it into the stream. Maybe I didn't release my hold on time, but I hurtled down along with it and found myself in the water with the log above me.

It was my third fall within the last hour, and everyone found it amusing. There were about three feet of clear water now, and the fall did not hurt me, but the bruises from the previous falls stung, but I did not mind it much. Overall, I had a heavenly feeling as I felt the weightlessness in the water and savored the cool breeze that sent shivers throughout my body as it caressed my wet skin.

We spent the next day watching a worker leveling the plowed paddy field, balancing himself on a long rectangular wooden plank connected to a pole pulled by two bullocks. We asked for a ride and took turns, and I fell again in the mud many times.

Back in the house after bathing in the stream and lying in bed after supper, I couldn't help my mind swaying back to Bombay with its horrible memories, though interspersed with some good ones. But the last days there, culminating in my sister's death, were the most traumatic.

3. Bombay (Now Mumbai)

Life in Bombay had not been much to my liking. I've had my early studies in Kerala. The Kindergarten was a single-story building with wide verandas and a large courtyard in front.

Classes were over by afternoon, and I had lunch with my mother in the teacher's room of the high school on the same campus, where she taught Mathematics. I was to wait in the teacher's room till evening every day, till my mother took me back home. Many teachers would pet me and ask me many questions, to which I must have given very witty answers because I clearly remember their amusement and laughter on hearing my responses.

The only lingering memory of kindergarten is that of a very fair-skinned girl. Her mother was an Englishwoman married to a Malayali doctor. Her complexion fascinated me so much that I went and touched her forearm to see if it was real. She was a sturdy girl, as I found out when she gave me a hard push, and I hurtled down into the large dustbin in front of the verandah. As I scrambled out, I saw her walking away with a snort and an air of disdain.

"What happened? How did you get so dirty?" My mother was shocked when I reached there for lunch that day.

"I slipped and fell into the dustbin as I was walking along the edge of the veranda," I replied. The other teachers found this hilarious and laughed their hearts out, and I am sure my small lie might have saved many lives. If they had known the truth, they would have laughed to death.

After Kindergarten, the Primary School was a long, straight, single-story building like a shed, with wooden screens separating the classes. We could hear the lessons taught in the adjacent classrooms, which almost always seemed to be more interesting.

Classes were till evening, and lunch was again with mother in the teacher's room of the high school. I had to face taunts from classmates who teased me for being such a mama's boy. My mother refused when I requested her to give me a packed lunch, like all the others, and I left it at that. Lunch in the Teacher's room had its merits too, as all the teachers brought different dishes and some ordered it from a hotel. They shared all the side dishes, and I would get to eat a tasty variety.

When I had almost finished the second standard, my mother gave birth to Leelamol, her third child and only girl, and my father got transferred to Bombay. Already on maternity leave, she took a long break from school, and we all shifted to the big city.

Our home, the official residence of the church Vicar, called the Parsonage, was an extension of the church building. The ground floor had the dining-cum- sitting room and the kitchen, and the top floor had a large bedroom divided into two by a bookshelf. It opened to a corridor with the bathrooms and led to the staircase's landing through which we could get into the church's balcony. The church balcony was our playground except for Sundays when they laid out chairs for the church service people.

I joined a Catholic English-medium school. It was a massive three-storied building built of granite and bricks, painted a gloomy grey with the borders in white. I don't remember seeing a single tree anywhere in the extensive compound

My father took me to the Vice Principal's room, where many other priests and nuns were present, all dressed in chocolate brown robes. None of them looked at me but for an occasional cursory glance. They seemed more interested in my father, who too was in robes, albeit a white one. My father was a priest of a tiny Christian denomination in Kerala, supposed to be the descendants of those converted to Christianity by St. Thomas in the first century. And so it was that most of its members had Thomas in their names.

The Vice Principal asked me something, but I didn't know a word in English and could not understand his question. "Can't he understand even this simple question? How can we admit him here? Take him to a Hindi medium government school."

My father pleaded with them, saying I didn't know a single word of Hindi either. "He was a good student in our native school, where the lessons were in Malayalam. I'm sure he will pick up."

"He is a fellow priest, and we must help him." The Vice Principal seemed sympathetic while discussing with his colleagues. "We can try to admit him to a lower class."

"In that case, we can only admit him to lower kindergarten," one priest suggested.

"But that would put him back by four years!" My father was frantic by then. "He has completed the second standard and should now be in the third." After much wrangling, they agreed to admit me to the first standard.

Appachen (that's what I called my father) took me to school the first day. "Tomorrow onwards, come on your own. Take note of all the landmarks- you should not get lost. And be careful about the traffic. Walk on the footpath, and here, where you have to cross, wait till the traffic is clear and quickly walk across." He showed me the zebra crossing just in front of the school.

I was the tallest boy in the class, the leanest, darkest, as well as the oldest. As I sat in my chair and looked around, I saw the other children chatting in Hindi, though it was forbidden to speak Hindi in that English Medium School. Since I could understand neither, I just sat there in silence, fiddling with my bag, which contained my lunch box, a plastic water bottle, and some textbooks.

Realizing that I could not survive in school without learning the language, my parents switched to English at home. But the little English I learned with intensive coaching by my parents in the last two weeks seemed inadequate.

As everyone chatted away, I had a sinking, lonely feeling. The chatter stopped, and everyone stood up for a unified chant of 'Good Morning, Miss!' I caught on a bit late, and so I ended up repeating it alone at the end. Everyone turned to look at me, and subdued laughter spread in the class.

"Keep quiet!" The young teacher ordered and turned to me. "What is your name?" I was prepared for this one and answered promptly.

"How old are you?"

I knew this one too! "Eight years," I replied.

"How is it that you are eight years old and still in the first standard?" This was too much for me. I could make out what the teacher was asking, but I burst into tears, finding no way to reply. Some of my classmates were laughing, but others seemed concerned. Confused about how to deal with me, the teacher took me to the staff room, where many people tried to console me. I could not understand them but could make out just a few words like 'stop crying' and 'big boy.'

My class teacher became worried. She went out to find someone who could speak in Malayalam and brought him to the staff room. "Don't worry," he told me. "Your father will come to pick you up in the evening."

4. School in Mumbai

I set off for school alone the next day. Despite my mother's protests, my father was firm in his resolve to send me alone. I was not much worried about finding my way, but a fear nagged in my mind about the Marathi Sena. "They will kill you if they find out you are a Malayalee," some boys I met in church last Sunday had warned me. I asked my father about this, but he just laughed it off. "Yes, they resent us who are grabbing all the jobs, but they don't go about killing all Malayalees."

It was just about a kilometer from my house to the school, and in a few days, I became pretty confident, but I barely escaped with my life on the fifth day. I had not reached the zebra crossing but crossed the road there, seeing no traffic. I could see a truck approaching but reckoned I could make it if I dashed across and made a run for it.

It must have been a banana peel, but before I knew it, I slipped on something and fell flat right in the middle of the road. I could hear the squealing of brakes, and then there was darkness. I was under the truck, which had stopped. Before I could decide whether to crawl out, the vehicle started moving and sped away.

A crowd gathered around me. Some were shouting at me, but others looked at me with concern. I could not make out a word they were saying. A police officer helped me to my feet. I was shaking, though in one piece; the truck had passed harmlessly over me. I did not report this incident to anyone at school or at home, but I was more careful after that day.

Slowly, I got accustomed. Roger Benny was my classmate, sitting in the chair on my right. He would talk to me in English, so I had someone I could converse with. The only problem was that he was the bragging type, and I did not want to be seen as lacking. So when he said that his father owned two cars, I told him that my father had three. Roger Benny looked skeptical, so when he told me they had three bedrooms in their house, I played it safe, and so, with a sorrowful face, I admitted we had only two. Though it was often a 'my father is richer than yours' type of conversation, I was happy to have someone to talk to, at least in broken English. All the others would only speak in Hindi unless the teachers were around. My English improved because at home, it was always English for me.

The school had terrifying systems for enforcing discipline. I have never seen a match being played on the football field, but they used it to punish errant students. The usual method of punishment was to make the students crawl on their knees five times around the ground in the blistering sun. A more severe punishment was to tie the student bare-chested to a goalpost and cane his back. In one instance, an ambulance was called when a boy being thus punished passed out, and the teacher could not revive him.

There was an atmosphere of tension throughout the school. At intervals, the Principal stood watching the whole compound from the balcony on the second floor, which extended from his office. He was a formidable figure in his brown robes, with a large brass whistle hung from his neck. He would blow the whistle if he spotted any troublemaker, and everyone was supposed to stand still wherever they were. He would then point out the offender, and his trusted team of monitors would fetch the boy to punish him according to the seriousness of the offense.

Once, while strolling along the footpath, Arnab, always a troublemaker in my class, came in the opposite direction. "Hello, black giraffe," he called out to me. I was aware of this nickname, but nobody had called me so to my face. I got furious and gave him a hard push that sent him reeling to the ground. The shrill whistle sounded from above, and everyone stood still. I knew it was for me. I dashed into the school building, covering my face so that none would recognize me. I rushed into an empty classroom and sat panting in a chair. It was an impulsive reaction. Thinking about the consequences that would follow made me shiver. *I should have stood there! If they catch me, they will flog me on the goalpost.*

I heard voices. "He must be hiding in a classroom. Check each room." It was the Principal's gang searching for me! Frantically, I looked around. The massive teacher's desk on a platform on one side of the room had a large drawer at the bottom. I opened it just enough to get inside and squeezed myself into it. It was almost empty except for some chalk pieces and the duster.

I heard footsteps approaching. "This room also seems to be empty. Quick, check the other rooms. Once the bell rings and everybody gets back into the class, it will be difficult to find him!"

I could hear the beating of my heart and wondered if they would hear it too! The smell of the chalk powder was getting into my nose. Trying to suppress the mounting impulse to sneeze, I scratched my nose. I've heard you could subdue a sneeze that way, but the urge increased. I hoped they wouldn't notice the open drawer and decide to look inside.

"There is nobody here," someone shouted, and I could hear them move on. I crawled out from the drawer, cupped my hands over my nose and mouth, and let out the long-overdue sneeze. The bell rang, and the boys started streaming back into the classrooms, and I rushed to the corridor and joined them.

Sitting in class, I expected to be pulled up anytime. *Arnab would have told them it was I who pushed him! They will come for me any minute.* I couldn't concentrate in class. I could see Arnab two rows ahead, but he seemed least concerned.

The last bell rang, and nobody had called me. Maybe Arnab has not yet complained, and he might do so soon after class! I went up to him to apologize and plead not to complain about me.

Arnab smiled. "You know, they questioned me for some time, but I told them I didn't see who it was and did not know why he hit me. I knew it would be flogging on the goalpost for you if I tell, because you ran off after the whistle."

Arnab became my best friend in school. No bully dared intimidate me with him around.

5. Book Uncle

As with the school, the city evoked no fascination for me. It was a suffocating feeling. The air smelled of smoke, and my white shirt would turn grey by evening. The compulsory necktie added to the discomfort, and I had to constantly control my urge to loosen it, as a loose tie would invite punishment.

My father sometimes took us with him on weekends while visiting his parish members' homes. Mom stayed back home with my sister, still an infant. My attraction was the assortment of snacks they offered us, but the train journey was a horrifying experience. The railway station was just a short walking distance from my house. We got in and out of the train by merging into the crowd, which would carry you forward. My father would carry my younger brother on his shoulder, but I was left to fend for myself.

Getting out was more challenging, and you had to force yourself against those jostling to get inside. My father would hold my arm and pull me out through the wall of passengers. Many scrambled onto the train's roof when there were more passengers than the train would hold.

One fateful day, it was hectic, and the crowd was horrible. As the train screeched to a halt, I took a deep breath and braced myself for the onslaught. Some were already climbing up the roof. I saw sparks above me, and then there was the smell of burning hair and flesh. Screams rent the air as a young man fell from the roof onto the platform in a bundled heap, just in front of me.

The overhead line of the electric train had electrocuted him. People took care not to step on him while getting in or alighting from the train. We got in too, and soon the train was on its way, delayed by just a few minutes.

It was the house of a college professor. "I never see you in church on Sundays. Why don't you drop in once in a while?" my father asked him.

"What will I gain by coming there? I spend my time here reading. It's way better than spending the time inside the church and listening to those stupid sermons." He paused as though worried he had offended my father." Sorry. I didn't mean you. Anyway, I haven't heard any of your speeches."

I noticed his large bookshelf separating the living room from the dining area, full of neatly stacked books. Seeing my interest, he knelt in front of the bookshelf, pulled out a book from the lower rack, and gave it to me. "You can borrow this. I bought these books for my children when they were young. If you like it, I can give you more." I looked at the cover. 'The Famous Five,' by Enid Blyton. I lounged back on the sofa and started reading.

"Come to church this Sunday," my father urged Book Uncle ('That's the name I came to refer to him later.) "Please listen to my sermon, and later, tell me the silly things I've said." Book Uncle laughed as he replied, but I didn't hear him. I was immersed in the book.

Fatty, the young hero, was figuring out how to escape from the room where Goon, the police officer, had locked them in when my father nudged me. "Come, it is time for us to go." Reluctantly, I closed the book and got up.

"You have already read through that much? Great! You will finish it tonight." Book Uncle again knelt before the shelf and fished out two more books. "Take these too, and you can return them when I come to church this Sunday."

Sunday was four days away, and I could read and re-read all the books. Book Uncle brought three more books when he came to church on Sunday, and I grabbed them while returning the old ones. "You should tell him to concentrate on his studies as well. He is always engrossed in books," my father complained to Book Uncle.

6. Entertainment in Bombay

They had an enormous courtyard for the church, a wonderful playground for us, our house being a part of the chapel. But I had no friends to play with.

The adjoining plot was not exactly a slum, but it had seven dilapidated houses cramped together, with no walls or boundaries separating them. They were laborers working on nearby construction projects. They had a shared pond in the center, their water source, and the kids' swimming pool. As the boys frolicked in the water, I would watch from this side of the wall.

"Come on," one kid gestured to me. I longed to join them but did not have permission to cross over.

"Wait," I gestured back and ran back into the house to ask my father.

"But you can't swim!" my request startled Appachen.

"It's okay. They will teach me,"

"No, we don't know those people. And that pool looks dangerous." He was firm.

Crestfallen, I longed for the gay abandon those kids enjoyed but had to be content playing with my younger brother in and around the house. He was too small for me to play with, but we often played hide and seek.

One day, we began the game early when my mother had gone to visit a neighbor, carrying Leelamol. When it was my turn to close my eyes and count till fifty, I did a cheat sneak and saw him enter the wardrobe, closing the door behind him. Soon as I finished counting, I straightaway went to the closet. Instead of exposing him, I had a naughty idea. I turned the key from outside and locked him in. I grabbed a book and relaxed on the cot, waiting for him to call out and request me to open the cupboard.

After some time, he started thumping on the door, shouting at me to open the door. *Let him wait for some time more*. A few moments later, I thought it was time to let him out and went to open the wardrobe. I tried to turn the key, but it was stuck and wouldn't budge even though I made every effort. The thumping on the door became fainter, and the voice from within became muffled before it went silent.

Alarmed, I rushed downstairs to fetch Thankayyan, our helper. He was not in the kitchen. I ran out, calling, "Thankayyan! Thankayyan!" - loud enough for even the neighbors to hear. He was there in the courtyard, attending to the rose bushes. I told him about the situation, and he came running after me.

There was no sound from the wardrobe. "Are you sure he's inside?" Thankayyan asked while trying to open the lock, but it remained jammed. "I'll try to lubricate it with some oil," he shouted and ran downstairs to the kitchen.

He rushed back with a bottle of coconut oil, smeared the key with the oil, and tried again. It worked, and the door swung open. My brother lay still at the bottom with a bluish tinge on his face and lips. We pulled him out and lay him on the floor.

"Wake up!" Thankayyan shouted while tapping his cheeks, but he lay there with no response. "Rub his hands vigorously!" Thankayyan was doing the same on the soles of his feet. My brother still lay frightfully immobile. Thankayyan pinched his nose, and covering his mouth with his own, started blowing into him. He massaged his chest in between and kept repeating the procedure.

My brother started coughing and opened his eyes. He took in a few deep breaths. The bluish tinge gave way to a healthy pink, and he sat up, looking bewildered. Thankayyan saved the life of a prominent future personality in Kerala's political landscape that day.

We became excited when my father agreed to take us to a movie a few days later. It was an unorthodox decision for a priest, and many conservative parish members considered it sinful. The film was 'Tarzan and Jane,' and its effect on me was such, that I dreamed of swinging on vines through forests for several days.

Having learned about our escapade, a parish member asked my father about this. "I heard you had taken your family for a film? Is it appropriate, especially for a priest?"

"Certainly! It is excellent entertainment, and children should have the opportunity to watch wonderful films," Appachen replied.

"But where do you get to see decent films?" He was persistent. "Even in this film, Jane was not dressed properly!"

"So you have watched it too?"

"Err... no, I came to know from people who watched it."

I felt sure he was lying, considering the time he took to respond, but my father did not indicate that he disbelieved him.

7. Tragedy

Leelamol was growing fast, and she started taking baby steps. I enjoyed spending time with her, responding to her demands, which she conveyed by calling me 'Chacha,' and pointing to whatever needed my attention. When insistent, it went 'Chachachachacha!'

Somehow, I managed my two years of schooling in Bombay without further mishaps. The school had unorthodox methods for punishments and rewards. Minor offenses like not doing homework or giving wrong answers to questions in class would invite punishments like being made to stand in the corner of the classroom or doing ten to twenty sit-ups, holding your ear lobes.

A favorite with some teachers was coloring the nose with red ink and decorating the ears with flowers. She would then entrust the class monitor to take the offender to all the classrooms to be exhibited thus, and face the taunts. Once, a teacher stripped the boy from the waist down before taking him around to be displayed. There was a hue and cry, and his parents came to the school with a lawyer. The management avoided legal action by sacking the teacher.

One day, I feared the worst when the teacher called out, "Thomas, come here," while checking our assignments. Walking to the front of the class with a pounding heart, I felt relieved when I saw her smiling. She complimented my neat handwriting and wanted to reward me. She called the class monitor and told him to escort me to all the classes and display my assignment. "Make sure he gets a standing ovation in each class," she instructed him.

I walked with him from class to class, savoring in the praises of the teachers and the standing ovation accorded to me by the students on her instruction. After visiting about four to five classrooms, he got tired of it. *He prefers escorting those punished with reddened noses, enjoying their humiliation.* "Finished so soon?" the Teacher asked as we returned to our class. I nodded along with him. It was always better not to get into the bad books of the class monitor.

The music class was the one which I enjoyed most. The teacher was a pretty young Anglo-Indian lady who taught us 'Doe, a deer,' from 'The Sound of Music' and other popular country songs. We would then sing these songs, with the teacher accompanying us on the piano. I was rendering the piece, 'Old MacDonald had a farm,' with gusto, mimicking the sounds of all the animals on the farm, when the Teacher stopped the music and addressed me. "Please reduce your volume. I would like to hear the others also sing."

Smallpox was spreading and taking its toll in the locality, and a vaccination drive was on. Doctor Uncle was a parish member, and many in our church depended on him for medical advice. He insisted on everyone taking vaccines, but my father was not keen.

Sukumaran Vaidyar was a Malayalee and a proponent of

naturopathy who stayed near us. He advocated natural methods to treat all ailments and opposed all modern medical drugs. "Vaccines are lethal poisons injected into your body by these modern doctors,' he used to say. "Keep your children safe from them. It will cause cancers later on." We came to depend on Sukumaran Vaidyar for all our illnesses. He would advise some special diets and different herbs ground to an unpalatable paste that I loathed taking.

During the lunch interval at school, I would stray outside to see the bustle of vendors of ice cream and other delicacies who thronged the road next to the high wall of the compound. I watched greedily as the others bought and ate brightly colored ice sticks and other goodies. Pocket money was not something I enjoyed, and I felt resentful that my parents did not give me some, like most others.

There was a glass bowl on our bookshelf at home, where my parents kept the loose change. I pinched some cash and bought a paani-poori and an ice stick during the lunch break. It tasted so good that I couldn't resist the temptation the next day, and it went on thus every day till Appachen noticed the dwindling cash in the bowl. I denied any wrongdoing until he flogged the truth out of me.

That night, as I lay in bed, my whole body ached. The bruises from the intense lashing that I received were stinging, but apart from that, I felt drained and exhausted. I was too tired to go to school the next day and lay in bed, too weary even to get up for breakfast. By evening, when my father returned home, my mother informed him how I had vomited and had not taken lunch. My urine had changed to a dark yellow. Worried, father went to fetch Sukumaran Vaidyar. Feeling guilty, Appachen told him how he had punished me.

Sukumaran Vaidyar parted my eyelids with his thick fingers and looked into my eyes. "He has jaundice," he declared. "It's not because of your flogging, but by eating the contaminated junk food from the vendors outside his school. I will prepare some herbal medicines for him. He has to stay in bed and limit water intake to not more than half a glass a day."

My father followed Sukumaran Vaidyar's instructions to the letter and allowed me only a tablespoon of water each hour. That night, I felt famished as I lay awake. My tongue was parched and dry, and yearning for a sip, I crept downstairs to the kitchen to steal some water. I had reached halfway down the steps when Appachen, who somehow got wind of my attempt, caught up with me and hauled me back to bed. He consoled me with an extra half a tablespoon of water. After a grueling week, my condition improved, and I was allowed more water. Water never tasted so delicious.

Several years later, I learned that jaundice was the presenting symptom of many diseases, of which Viral Hepatitis was the most common. It was essential to stay well hydrated during the illness, and I should consider myself lucky to have survived the torture of unscientific treatment.

The final exams for the second standard were near when tragedy struck. Leelamol was running a fever, and the medicines my father had given her didn't seem to work. Small blisters appeared all over her body. Sukumaran Vaidyar was unavailable as he was in a large modern hospital ICU with a severe stroke.

Appachen requested Doctor Uncle to see her when he attended church service on Sunday. One look at her, and he asked. "Have you not vaccinated her against Smallpox?"

"No, I've never believed in vaccines," my father replied.

"You mean to say that none of these children are vaccinated?" The doctor was reproachful. "This girl almost certainly has Smallpox, and she has to be admitted to the hospital under strict isolation. And plan to get the other children vaccinated soon!"

They took her to the hospital in an ambulance, and I never saw her alive again.

The tragedy evoked in me an intense dislike for Sukumaran Vaidyar and his unscientific methods and a desire to be like Doctor Uncle, who might have been able to prevent this death if he had had his way and got us all vaccinated early.

8. Valiammachi

For Valiammachi, our home was her kingdom, and nothing could compare. Our uncle, her eldest son, had once taken her abroad to Kuwait, hoping to give her a break from the lonely life at home. She created such an uproar there that she had to be sent back on the next available flight. "What country is this, where you don't even get a fresh coconut?" She was livid with her justification.

Whenever I got a few holidays, I pestered my parents to let me visit Valiammachi. We got an extended stay with so many cousins during the Christmas holidays. We roamed the fields, singing carols at the top of our voices.

The stark green of the paddy fields had taken on a yellowish tinge, and the grains had sprouted. Swarms of green parrots flew in to feast on them, and we had a great time chasing them off. The firecrackers we were allowed to scare them off were a boon that we enjoyed. Lighting the wick of the explosives, which came in pieces of coconut leaves wrapped into a small triangle, we hurled them into the field and watched as the birds flew off in hordes, like a green flying carpet, as it exploded.

The next time I came to visit, it was the harvesting season. Rows of women bent down, cutting the sheaves of paddy with sickles. Tied up into bundles, they stacked them up in the corner of the field. They separated the grains by trampling them under their feet. Placing chest-high a wooden log on stilts, the workers lined up on either side, leaning on it with their arms while threshing the paddy sheaves with their legs in rhythm to country songs. The grains were collected and heaped high on woven grass mats spread out on the fields.

We children guarded the valuable grains against thieves at night, lying in makeshift huts of thatched coconut leaves, with just the croaking of frogs and chirping of crickets breaking the stillness of the night. We burned incense to keep mosquitos away but had to suffer bites by some hardy ones who ignored the smell over the inviting scent of human blood.

When they harvested sugarcane, they extracted the juice with a machine that ran on ox power. The device's handle was a long wooden pole, turned by a bull walking in circles around it with the other end of the rod tied on its shoulder. We took turns climbing on the pole for a free merry-go-round. Unless we balanced ourselves on the bar, we would tumble down to the soft ground.

We spent most of our time under the colossal country mango tree just near the edge of the high land before the paddy fields. We waited for the next gust of wind to send down a shower of mangoes. The wind would sometimes shy away for a long time, and after a prolonged wait, we would get frustrated and resort to voodoo tricks.

The surest way to induce the wind to blow on the tree was to catch a carpenter ant, lock it up inside a jackfruit leaf, and nail it onto the tree's trunk. Once our wish was fulfilled with a gust of wind and a few dropped mangoes, we took the leaf out and unfolded it for the ant to happily scramble away to freedom. Then, if the wind took too long to blow again, we started afresh with a new ant and leaf. Time flew. Munching the sweet mangoes and waiting for the next lot, nobody bothered about lunch. But Valiammachi was strict about getting back home before dark.

Getting up in the mornings was a cumbersome task. While still in bed, half awake, we could hear Valiammachi at work. Her first task was churning the curd to skim out the butter. She used a gadget, a wooden spatula with spokes at one end, immersed in the earthen pot containing the curd. She entwined the top end with two loops of a thin rope just above where she kept her feet on the pot, with another rope tied between her big toes, which provided a fulcrum for the spatula. 'Swish - Swish,' she would go on, pulling each end of the rope to turn the spokes both ways, churning up the curd. The milk and curd from our house were so popular that people all around came to buy them.

Ours was one of the wealthiest households in our village, which only meant that we could afford enough food to fill our stomachs all three times a day. Being landlords, people addressed my grandparents respectfully as 'Thampuran' and 'Thampuratti.' Once, when I was sitting on our veranda with my brother, someone came asking for Thampuratti. Never having heard the word before, I told him I did not know, while my brother went to Valiammachi and asked her, "Where is this thing Thampuratti kept? Somebody is asking for it!"

But frugality was the watchword. My father told me that while he was a school student, to save oil, studying with the kerosine lamp's light was not allowed, and he had to get up early in the mornings to catch the first rays of sunrise to read his books.

My grandfather had not been keen on his children studying much, and he preferred them to help in the fields and reduce hired labor costs. So much so that when his eldest son passed out from school and was ready to join college, he denied permission. 'It's a sheer waste of money.'

Frustrated, my uncle left home one day to seek his pastures. After working for some time in the Navy, he migrated abroad, riding across the seas with other fortune seekers in a dingy and reaching the shores of Kuwait. He lived in a tent pitched in the desert till he got a regular job on the mainland. He was a keen learner and a hard-working employee and soon rose to become a store manager in an American oil company. Uncle was thus a pioneer among the hordes of Malayalees who migrated to the Gulf countries in subsequent years to earn their living and contribute a significant chunk of the state's revenue.

When my grandfather passed away, my uncle took it upon himself to care for the family and educate his younger siblings. Thus my father could join college and do his Pre-degree in far-off Changanachery. Though eligible for a regular degree course, he preferred to pursue Theology. After graduating, they ordained him as a priest in our church- a matter of great prestige for the family.

Valiammachi had her hands full, especially when all of us, her grandchildren, were visiting. She never tired of making many delicacies for us. Goodies like flavored ripe bananas fried in coconut oil, different vadas (a savory doughnut), and meat cutlets accompanied the evening tea daily. Even the typical breakfast and dinner were delicious dishes once she had worked her magic on them.

On rare occasions, we had chicken. Valiammachi would make the grand announcement and point out the cock we had to catch for slaughter. We ran after the obstinate fowl, chasing it all over the property, till one of us nabbed it and handed it over to an uncle for execution. The person successful would be an instant hero.

Valiammachi would hoard all seasonal edibles to last for the entire year by preserving them in various ways. Tapioca cut into small pieces were boiled and sun-dried to be stocked. She made mango bars by drying the pulp with spices and spread out on grass mats to keep them in the sun for several days. Ripe bananas laced with condiments were likewise dried and preserved. She stored these dried fruits in large air-tight tin cans on the spacious wall shelves of the dining room. Valiammachi occasionally doled out these delicacies, but we pilfered them whenever possible.

Kochettan was the expert lifter. There was a large den at the bottom of the shelf with a steel rod on top, from which Valiammachi hung fresh ripe bananas. Sliding open the shelf door, he would crawl in and sit inside, devouring them until he could take no more. Valiammachi sometimes rushed in from the kitchen, hearing the shelf door open, but he would have slid the door back shut, and she never suspected he was inside.

The clucking sound from the poultry coop near the cattle shed was the proud proclamation of a hen that it had just laid an egg. Valiammachi would finish whatever she was doing in the kitchen and rush to collect it, but often she would get only the empty eggshells. Kochettan liked his eggs raw and would beat her to it.

So also with milk. Kochettan would scoff at us, who drank our milk when Valiammachi gave it boiled and with sugar. He preferred to sit beside the cow grazing in the fields, catch its teats, and milk it straight into his mouth. The aim might not always be perfect, and he would get milk all over his face. Valiammachi chased him off with a long cane when she caught him red-handed (rather white-faced).

She often had this cane to discipline us, but I don't remember a single instance when she had brought it down on anyone. I had a feeling that she also enjoyed our antics.

We liked to delay waking up in the mornings as much as possible. "It's almost afternoon, and none of you plan to get up?" She would ask while prodding us awake. We lined up in the kitchen, getting up from bed and finishing the morning ablutions.

"Is breakfast ready, Valiammachi? We are hungry."

"The sun has barely risen, and you already want breakfast?" she would shout back, unmindful that she had declared it almost afternoon just a few moments ago.

She had her rules set out and was angry when anyone broke them. I woke up one day when I heard her angry voice shouting at her son, our youngest uncle, who often joined us in some of our games. He was also the most studied among his siblings and worked as a professor at a college in Kochi. "You people don't know the value of money. You are now a college professor! When are you going to learn?"

I wondered what serious crime he had committed. As no ripe bananas were available at home, he had gone out and bought a bunch from the nearby shop. He had broken the cardinal rule that all the food we eat should only be from our property.

9. Dr. Kampu

It was Valiyammachi who first called me a doctor. 'Dr. Kampu' was the nickname by which she called me. 'Kampu' was the Malayalam word for a twig or stick, and I, being skinny, justified the name, but I was clueless about why she prefaced it with the title of 'Doctor.' But somehow, it kindled in me a desire to become one.

One day, she came to me holding the newspaper she was reading. "See this!" she said, pointing to a news column. "A patient has died a few days after surgery. They did a postmortem and found that the doctor had left a pair of scissors in his abdomen! You should be very careful when you become a doctor."

My absent-mindedness was always a concern with her and a scandal among my cousins. The other day, while playing shuttlecock, the shuttle landed on the terrace, and I was sent up to fetch it. Climbing up the wooden staircase to the attic and crawling down to the balcony, I stood there, having forgotten why I climbed up. Valiammachi was horrified at hearing this story and expressed her anxiety.

The days of bliss ended abruptly. I knew it when, after waking up, I looked out of the window and saw my mother walking up the path to the house. My heart sank; I knew she had come to fetch me back to her home in Thiruvalla.

"It's two weeks now, and you have still not thought of returning? The school will reopen in another week!" she addressed me with her voice raised. She allowed me two days more after my fervent pleadings, aided by Valiammachi's recommendation.

Life in my mother's family house in Thiruvalla was a placid affair. My grandfather had a shelf stacked with old issues of Reader's Digest, and I went through them all, starting from one end of the top rack. Grandpa constantly chewed paan, which stained his lips and mouth a permanent deep red. He was a retired headteacher of a government school and was a stickler for order and discipline. While taking me out for long treks in the evenings, Grandpa followed the same route every day, so there was no variety. He narrated stories as we walked, but often repeated them several times.

All his stories would end with a moral. A favorite with him was the story of 'The boy who stood on the burning deck.' The boy was the son of a sailor. When the ship docked in a harbor, the father asked his son to stay at a specific spot on the ship's deck until he returned, when he went out for some shopping. The vessel caught fire, and everyone escaped through the boat's walkway to the harbor.

"Come on, quick! This ship will burn!" Many called him while passing the gangway, but the boy did not budge, and he stood there and got burned to death.

"That was very foolish of him! He should have run to safety," I remarked.

"But then he would disobey his father." My grandfather seemed to justify his action, and I thought it better not to argue.

My grandfather's bath was a daily ritual involving the whole family- an elaborate affair that would take him an hour and another hour of preparations that preceded the actual bath for us. The large copper vessel used would take almost a whole barrel of water. Filling this took quite some time, with water drawn from a deep well adjoining the house. The bathroom was a good fifty meters away, in a separate single-room building. (The toilet was another hundred meters away, keeping with the tradition of those times.)

It was a day of great rejoicing for all when Grandpa installed a pump to draw water from the well. We filled the vessel with water and boiled it with many leaves and herbs. I remember neem, tamarind, pepper, and jackfruit leaves, but there were many more.

The bathroom was built in such a way that we could light a fire under the vessel from outside. We doused the fire once the water had boiled for at least ten minutes. It was then kept to cool down to the right warmth. It was my task to keep testing the temperature until it was right. When done, I would take a sample in a mug and bring it to him to check. He would wait prepared, smearing medicated coconut oil all over his body. If satisfied, he would proceed to the bathroom. "Let it cool for some time more," he would often say, but when he thought the water had cooled too much, it was tedious to light the fire again and repeat the entire process.

Saturday was Beggar's Day. Grandfather would sit on the veranda with a bowl of one-paise and two-paise coins. The beggars would come in a steady stream, starting early morning, and the ritual will be over by afternoon. Once he ran out of change, he would take out a twenty-five paise coin and get it changed from a beggar who would get one paisa extra for the service. As the years went by and inflation rose, he hiked the minimum dole to two paise.

Fish was an absolute necessity for all meals, and a heavy pall of gloom would fall if it were unavailable on any day. Twenty-five paise fetched enough fish for two meals for the whole family. Mackerel was the standard sea fish purchased from the market, for which I would go with the money. I could get twenty-five fish for this amount, and if the fish were small, even up to fifty.

Often, we bought the freshwater fish brought daily by the vendor. The ferocious haggling over the price was excellent entertainment for me. Occasionally, the lady would get too offended and walk off in a huff gathering up all the fish back into her basket, only to return some time later with a 'last-price offer,' over which there would be further bargaining. I cannot recall when they didn't strike an agreement and a sale did not happen.

Once they complete the deal, there will be a truce, and everyone will be back to friendly mode. The lady will stay around to clean the fish and cut it into neat pieces, sipping on the tea served to her and exchanging gossip.

When they planned to make 'Appam' (delicious pancakes made from fermented rice dough), they would give me an extra fifty paise to buy toddy on the way back from the market. Toddy was the popular local alcoholic beverage used for fermenting dough, and it was taboo for a conservative family like ours, except for fermentation purposes. I could hear the raunchy jokes and the lewd conversation inside the shop while waiting outside for my order.

I always wondered why they asked me to buy fifty paise worth of it, when we needed just a tiny quantity for the appam, and where the rest of it disappeared.

Despite such entertainment, it was boring for me at my mother's house, and I longed for the school to reopen.

10. Countryside School

The school did not have any rules about uniforms. We would wear a shirt and shorts, or sometimes a 'mundu' (a white cloth wrapped around the waist to cover the legs).

I wore the plain shirts stitched by the local tailor who meticulously took our measurements. "Come after two weeks," he would say. When I went on the exact date, the shirt would not be ready, and he would announce the next date for delivery. It would take several such visits before he delivered the dress.

My chappals were also custom-made from leather by the local cobbler, who would sketch the outline of my footprint on a sheet of white paper and stack them into a folder with my mother's name written on it. The delivery was just like, or worse than, the tailor. Wearing new chappals inevitably caused blisters on my feet, which appeared in a few days and took several weeks to heal into a callus.

Occasionally, we got to wear the foreign shirts my aunts and uncles brought. My mother's eight siblings were abroad or working outside the state, and my father also had eight siblings, among which only three were in India. Visits from my uncles and aunts were exciting events for me. They came with heavy trunks packed with presents for all the relatives. I used to get new designer shirts, pens, pencils, rubber erasers, and pencil cutters.

The shirts would always be too short or too loose for me. Seeing that my brother always got well-fitting shirts was frustrating, but I couldn't blame anyone. They would never have imagined such a tall, skinny boy when they made custom sizes. Though the shirts were off-size, they were colorful, and I was glad to wear them to school.

It was a mixed school, but there was no interaction with the opposite sex. I learned the hard way that just borrowing a pen or smiling at a girl would create a major scandal. Not so with the teachers. Many of them would flirt openly in the staff room! A few boys swore to have seen some in compromising positions amongst the dark corners of the long passages connecting the classrooms.

While enrolling in school, my mother took me to the Headmaster to present my case. Though I had just completed the 2nd standard in Bombay, age-wise, I was eligible for the 5th standard.

Chacko Sir was an aged veteran who was due to retire next year. He wore spotlessly white jubbah and mundu and chewed paan. His lips and mouth were red as blood with betel quid, which he spat out at intervals into the large bronze spittoon kept by his side. "Let him be in standard five now. We can register him for the final exams in March." He paused for a spit and continued. "If he clears that, he can join as a regular student in the 6th standard from next year onwards. Meanwhile, let him take the English proficiency test to be selected for the English medium."

Being in the English medium was a prestigious affair. Our school had five divisions for each grade, of which only one division was for English medium, the rest being for Malayalam. They named the classes from A to E; the A division was for English medium. They based the selection on a test to assess skills in English. Coming from an English Medium School in Bombay, the test was a walk-over for me.

I thus joined class 5 A in school, not having seen 3rd and 4th grades. I did pretty well in my studies, but my mother tongue became my most vulnerable weak point. My peers had been learning Malayalam since they started school and could not comprehend my ignorance of the language. Students in the English medium had just one paper for Malayalam in the examinations, but that became a monumental challenge for me. I could converse with my classmates in my mother tongue, but I found Malayalam was Greek to me in reading and writing.

I performed well in the science subjects but poor in languages, except English. I was always first in English but scored poorly in Hindi and failed Malayalam. My parents became worried and arranged for special tuition.

In the year-end examinations, I passed with good marks overall, but just the minimum pass mark for Malayalam, obviously the result of final moderation. I was now a regular student in class 6 A.

We could play with abandon during the intervals, especially the one-hour-long break in the afternoon. We would gulp down our lunches as quickly as possible and rush out of the classrooms. The girls seemed more interested in enjoying their lunch. By the time we finished lunch, they would not even have started, inspecting the different dishes in each other's tiffin boxes and sharing them.

Our favorite game was 'Thieves and Police.' We divided ourselves into two gangs- P. C.'s and Praveen's team and alternated each day to be the thieves and police. PC and Praveen, the best students in class, were the leaders, though, by themselves, both were not too good at games.

The fight was intense, but there was no hand-to-hand stuff. We were to pelt each other with missiles. The only approved missiles were the dry seeds of the large pine trees, of which there were plenty on the grounds. The first five minutes were for gathering the weapons and arming ourselves. We would stuff our pockets full with the pine seeds. We would bombard the opposing team with them at the signal from the referee (chosen from among the weak guys who would like to opt-out from the actual fight).

The school bell was the signal for the ceasefire. The referee would declare the winner, and we would rush back into the classrooms, quarreling about the results.

Fridays were different. There were no games on Fridays because we had the afternoon prayer meetings in the church. Chandy Sir was the person in charge. Participation was supposed to be voluntary, but Chandy Sir would come to the ground wielding a long cane and drive us all into the church like sheep. Some of the cleverer ones would run first into the church, and by the time Chandy Sir reached and started the prayer, they escaped through the windows on the opposite side.

Chandy Sir was more insistent with Christian boys. I was not aware of the religious identity of my friends, except by the obvious Christian names like Mathew, George, or Thomas, of which there were plenty. But the selective targeting of Christian students herded into church exposed Mohan as a Hindu while Sasi was a Christian. My mother being a teacher in the same school, it was hard for me to scoot from church. I gritted my teeth and bore the formality of the service, trying to ignore the wild screams of those playing outside. I would have given anything then to have been born a Hindu. It would also mean I wouldn't have to attend church every Sunday.

Mother was very strict with church attendance. She once forced me to attend church, though I was unwell. I fainted during service and had to be carried out to the veranda. The fresh air outside was enough to revive me.

However, I was among the fortunate few whose parents were not strict about returning home soon after school. That meant I had an hour for games after class. Games in the evening were more professional, like football or cricket, unlike the Thieves and Police games in the afternoon.

Those with cash pooled their resources to buy a rubber ball. (Some boys with more liberal parents allowed them to have pocket money, but I was not one of them.) It served as both a cricket ball and a football, depending on which game we played. One such ball would last two to three weeks if we were lucky. Once it developed cracks and the air inside had fizzled out, it would bounce no more, and we gave up playing cricket till we got a new ball with enough bounce. But we would play football with the floppy mass until it broke into pieces.

We kept two piles of school bags at both ends of the ground wide apart to indicate the goalposts. On returning home one day, my mother looked at me in surprise and asked, "Where is your school bag?"

I realized I had left it on the school grounds, still a goalpost, long after the game had ended. I rushed back to school, and my bag was there, a lonely object on the vast ground. This was just one instance of the forgetfulness for which I became infamous.

As there were no side or top bars for the goalposts, the umpire declared a goal at his discretion. It led to several disputes, which we resolved after heated arguments. Such disputes never ended unsolved, as everyone wanted to continue with the game.

Controversies in cricket were more challenging to resolve. Nobody wanted to become an umpire and be out of the game, so we changed the rules to have different umpires for each inning. Number eleven of the batting side played referee until he went in to bat when the batsman who had got out first would take his place. All umpiring decisions favored batsmen.

The problem got solved when we appointed Sasi as the permanent umpire. When he came to bat, he nominated the person to replace him. His love of sports meant he was unforgiving of any lapse by this stand-in umpire, even if the decision favored him. He preferred to walk than take advantage of a wrong decision that ruled him not out.

Sasi was a senior to most of us and became our classmate because he failed exams last year. He supplied the cricket bats for us. His father, a carpenter, made them, crafted from petioles, the thick stump of the coconut frond. These were so good that there were no takers when someone brought a proper cricket bat. Sasi's bats were much lighter and springy.

11. A Ghostly Encounter

Before I got into high school, my father finished his term in Bombay and was posted to a church in Kuttapuzha, a village on the outskirts of Thiruvalla. We made the last trip to Bombay to come back together after visiting Leelamol's grave. The three-day train trip is still fresh in my memory, though I had made these trips to Bombay many times earlier. Maybe I was too young then to remember. The window seats were ours by right, but I quarreled with my brother over who got the chair facing the back of the train. The one facing front had to contend with soot and bits of coal from the steam engine getting into his eyes.

Appachen had been on a shopping spree, buying all gadgets like a refrigerator, bread toaster, electric iron, and many other such stuff. "I have spent all my savings and got these items," he said. "It might be difficult to get these in Kerala." He packed them in three large crates to be shipped to our new address.

We said goodbye to all the parishioners and other friends. Many remarked that I had grown much since they last saw me. Book Uncle gifted me three books.

Leelamol's grave was in the public cemetery- a vast expanse of land dotted with crosses and marble statues of angels in various postures. We lay flowers at her tiny, modest grave with a simple cross and returned with my mother sobbing inconsolably.

"You should have taken a full ticket for this boy," the Train Ticket examiner (TTE) argued with my father on the train while coming back.

"But he has not completed twelve years! There are still three months to go," Appachen responded.

"Don't try to fool me," the TTE snapped back, looking at my face. "Boys don't sprout a mustache till they reach fourteen. Unless you can show me a certificate proving his age as less than twelve, I have to impose a fine."

My father took out his letter pad, wrote a certificate for my age, and handed it to him without another word. The TTE glanced through it and left without further arguments. (Back then, birth certificates issued by priests were valid documents.)

Upon returning, we settled in the new parsonage just behind the church. We arranged the furniture, leaving spaces for the gadgets in the consignment from Bombay, but there was no word from them even after a week. Inquiries revealed that the transportation company had gone bankrupt, and somebody had stolen all the shipments in transit. There was nothing to do but suffer the loss, as Appachen had not insured the freight.

School resumed as before, as also the games on the grounds. After the games, I would head home three kilometers away with Mathew Kurien (MK for short), who lived a bit further. The walk was eventful. We interacted with all the dogs and cats on the way. We also would buy cheap crackers. The ones called 'Potash' were the most affordable. These were rolls of thin paper strips with the ammunition packed at one-centimeter intervals in small bulges. These were loaded onto the magazine of a revolver and fired in succession. The gun we had developed snags, but we didn't have the money to buy another one, so we satisfied ourselves by exploding them, keeping the strip on a rock, and hitting the bulges on it with another stone.

The 'throw-crackers' were more fun, though costly. They would explode when hurled against a hard surface. If the throw were not forceful enough, it would bounce off unexploded. We would target the walls by the sides or sometimes straight down on the tarred road. One such missile did not explode, bounced off the road into a shop, and disappeared inside a vast pile of clothes stacked high on the floor. It was a laundry shop.

The shop owner was not amused as we went in and asked him if we could retrieve it. He rushed out as if it was a bomb inside. "Now, you better find it and get it out. If it explodes and damages any garment, you will pay for it."

We rushed out, having fished out our prized treasure from among the pile of clothes, ignoring his questions about our whereabouts. We were sure he had the evil intent of reporting to our parents. Being the Vicar of the nearby church just a few hundred meters away from his shop, he would know my father.

Our Parsonage, the official residence of the Vicar, was just behind the church. My father left no bit of the land around the compound idle, cultivating many types of vegetables. A high wall separated it from the church's cemetery on one side of this vegetable plot. The tapioca growing near the border produced such big tubers, and the snake gourds were so enormous that my mother was sure the corpses buried on the other side of the wall fertilized them. She refused to consume anything harvested from there.

The cemetery was my favorite spot for reading and studying. Being brought up without superstitions, I had no cause for worry while lying over the grave of the Late Lt. Col. Mathew Abraham. It had a marble sculpture of an open Bible in front of the granite cross, making it very convenient for me to lean back and rest my head at the foot of the cross.

The high wall around the cemetery had just one narrow exit. I could see the elevated railway track beyond the wall, and an occasional passing train was a welcome diversion. My friends in school were amazed to hear about my 'study room' and admired me for my absence of fear. "What is there to fear from dead people?" I would ask. "It is the living ones you have to be careful about."

I carried a novel with me into the cemetery, apart from the textbook and a notebook. When studies got too boresome, I switched to the story to relax. Often, I would complete two or three novels by the time I finished a chapter of the textbook. Once, while thus engrossed in a gripping ghost story, I got the fright of my life.

It was late into twilight, and I was straining my eyes to read the book when I noticed a ghastly white flare of light from the far end of the cemetery. It was not Billy, our cat, whose eyes glowing in the cemetery's darkness was familiar to me, even though it gave me a minor scare the first time. Watching mesmerized, I saw similar flames flaring up and fizzling out on and off from different directions, with the heavy black cloud of smoke spewed out from the coal engine of the train that had just passed, spreading an eerie background. I felt a tense uneasiness and retreated to the safety of our house.

I must have looked flustered because my father asked me, "Why did you rush into the house? You look as if you have seen a ghost!"

I recounted my encounter with the mysterious flashes in the cemetery.

"So, did you think they were ghosts? Do you believe such things exist?"

"Of course not!" I tried to be bold but sounded sheepish.

"Then why didn't you go close and see what it was?"

"I didn't think straight," I replied, feeling even more awkward. "I'll go now and see."

"No need. It's dark now, and you have to be careful about snakes. I will tell you what you saw." My father had a ready rational explanation. "You remember the heavy rains we had last week? It must have eroded the topsoil and exposed some bones of bodies buried there. Bones contain lots of Phosphorus which will burn when exposed to air." The next time I saw the flares, I had a good look.

12. Satisfaction for Men of Action

We received the once-in-a-blue-moon school tours with great excitement. I was among the fortunate few whose parents allowed their children to participate. We did not mind any of the hardships or discomfort. The buses taken on hire for the tour were rickety old ones past their prime. They enhanced the capacity by fixing two wooden benches longitudinally between the two rows of seats. Sixty children with two teachers- one male and the other female, cramped into the forty-seater bus. All these discomforts were of no relevance compared to the thrill of taking part in the excursion.

The tour had almost got canceled. The previous evening, we had all assembled in the school where we were to spend the night sleeping on the benches in the classrooms and set out very early in the morning. Being very excited about the trip and having the rare chance to spend the night with our friends, we chattered along till well past midnight before falling asleep, only to be woken up an hour later by the teachers. "Everyone, get ready! We have to leave immediately. And don't make any noise; otherwise, we will cancel the tour."

The Bishop's Palace, which housed the church's supreme head, was in the same sprawling compound. His Grace Thimothios Mar Athanasios, second in line to the church's supreme authority, was lying there on his deathbed in a coma for over two weeks. They discharged him from the hospital with nothing more to be done, and he lay there with everyone waiting for the inevitable end.

A steady stream of visitors came daily to pay their last respects to the dying patriarch. They took all the students from the school there in batches, and I had my turn just a few days back. We stood in a queue, moving forward at a snail's pace till we reached the expansive room with the bishop lying motionless on a bed in the middle, a plethora of tubes connected to him. The atmosphere was solemn and serene. Smoke from a bowl of burning incense filled the room, and there was constant chanting of devotional hymns and prayers by a group of priests in white robes seated at the head end of the bed in a semicircle.

I felt a sudden urge to relieve myself and went to the adjoining washroom. Two priests were there talking to each other, unaware of my presence. "How many days more will we have to keep up this horrible vigil? Can't the guy just call it quits and kick the bucket? I am near breaking point."

"It's that doctor attending on him creating this problem," the other priest replied. "Every time Thirumeni gets worse, and on the verge of death, he will administer a few injections and prolong his life. I think that doctor is looking for some publicity." (Thirumeni- meaning His Holiness, was how bishops were referred to.)

I left the washroom quietly, not wanting to embarrass the priests by letting them know I had been privy to their conversation. The episode shattered my feeling of awe with the solemn scene.

"Now, get going fast! Pack up your belongings and get on the bus." The teachers were frantic. It so happened that Thirumeni had passed away just some time back, and they wanted us to leave before the official announcement reached the school. They were concerned about the criticism they would have to face if it was known that they had taken us for an excursion on the day that Thirumeni died. They had already made all arrangements for the tour and our stay at different locations, and putting it off at the last moment would create many difficulties and loss of money.

We responded with absolute obedience, boarding the bus while talking to each other only in whispers. Everyone heaved a sigh of relief as we exited the compound through the main gate and soon burst into songs, which we continued till exhaustion overtook us, and we fell asleep heaped upon each other in the cramped space. The driver parked the bus for a few hours to catch some sleep and get us back to the original schedule.

Once we started climbing the tortuous road with many hairpin bends to Ootty, the famed hill station, the pungent smell of burning diesel was too unbearable, and nausea took over. Some started vomiting, starting a chain reaction until almost everybody had thrown out their entire stomach contents. There was a mad rush for the side seats to puke out from the bus, and when all the side seats were exhausted, the bus stopped for a vomiting break.

Once we reached Ootty, all tiredness vanished in the hill station's cool climate, and we resumed our persistent excited chatter. The Ootty Gardens was intoxicating with its extravagance of flowers with colors and smells of all hues. We never tired of rolling down the grassy slopes of the manicured lawns, then climbing back to roll down again.

Coming out of the gardens, we wandered around the marketplace. I bought a green fruit that I had never seen before. It was a pear. Taking a bite, I felt the fabulous texture and the exquisite taste, and I thought it was the tastiest fruit I had ever eaten. I bought half a dozen to take home with the bit of pocket money I had.

Some of my friends were puffing away on cigarettes, glancing around to ensure no teacher was watching. "Want a drag? It feels so good in this cool climate. It warms you from the inside!" MK generously offered me the fag he had been puffing on. I felt tempted. Every day, I used to see pictures on the front page of newspapers of handsome guys puffing away, surrounded by adoring beautiful ladies. 'SATISFACTION FOR MEN OF ACTION' was the catchline. But then, an image of my parents peering at me, as if to see what I'll do, flashed through my mind. I politely declined.

A few days after returning from the tour, my mother glared at me when she asked angrily. "You have disgraced your father and me! Why did you smoke cigarettes while you were on tour?"

I looked at her with my mouth wide open. "How can you say that? I didn't smoke even though many of my friends did."

"Don't try to fool me with that surprised look," she replied. "I came to know from a teacher who saw you!"

"Tell me which teacher. I will ask her." Despite my vehement denials and my persistent demands to know the teacher who reported this, she didn't seem to believe me and wouldn't divulge the teacher's name.

The narrow strip of land behind the large auditorium in the school compound that separated it from the football field below was where the students got together for all the unlawful pursuits-

smoking, sharing pornographic books, and some even engaging in homosexual activities. It was an unwritten rule that the last group was left to themselves and not be disturbed. Curiosity often led me to beg for a glimpse of the 'small books'- as they called the porn books and magazines that were the proud possession of some.

MK was puffing away on a cigarette. I wondered what it would be like and asked him for a drag. *Anyway, my mother thinks that I smoke.* The first drag had me in a fit of violent coughing. "Not so hard!" MK urged. "Take it slow, and don't inhale in too much." I got the hang of it and returned the fag after a few more drags. My head seemed to spin.

It went on thus for a few more days until I got the feeling MK was becoming reluctant to share. I saved some money, buying just a refill instead of an actual pen, saving all the scrap paper, and binding them together to avoid purchasing a rough book until I had enough to buy a few cigarettes. I was hooked.

13. Sir Isaac Newton and David Sir

All the boys (and a few girls too) had nicknames, usually unflattering, but we called each other by these names unless they were too insulting. These nicknames were apt and unique, and mine was 'Socrates.' I was confused about how this name suited me until Makri, the frog (Rajan in the school records), gave me the rationale. "You are brilliant, wise, and intelligent, but quite ugly- just like Socrates." I wondered whether to be proud or ashamed. Anyway, I continued to respond to whoever addressed me as Socrates cheerily. Over time, it got shortened to Soccer and just Socs.

I remember 'Kanthari' (Malayalam for bird's-eye chili), the fiery little puny girl with a sharp tongue. The nickname given to Mohan, the boy with one leg weak and shriveled because of Polio, was 'One point five.' It was very unkind, and I never used it, nor could I tolerate anyone who did. Only very few were insensitive enough to call him thus.

Mohan strutted along with the aid of a walking stick he held in his arms with his useless leg wrapped around it. As a result, he had mighty arms. He used to get enraged when called by his nickname, but those taunting him kept a safe distance. I found it difficult to tolerate such rudeness, so I would grab the offender and cling to him for just enough time for Mohan to strut across and rain powerful blows on the poor fellow with his muscular arms. All who wanted to tease him ensured I was not around when they taunted him. Though a skinny, weak guy, I would ward off any bullying with an intense fight, unmindful of the blows that fell on me, that even the notorious bullies were wary of confronting me.

My father got transferred again as the Principal of a Theological Institute, which was very near Mohan's house, so we returned together after school. He would take long strides, keeping his cane so far ahead for each step that it was difficult for me to keep pace.

Most teachers had nicknames like 'Machi' for Leelamma Teacher, but we students only used these names between us.

'Newton' was David Sir, our science teacher, who instilled awe and wonder in our classes, demonstrating each theory with relevant experiments. He had his share of eccentricities and could never agree with Newton's Laws, and Sir would explain his own ideas while reminding us to stick to Newton for our exams.

He would keep the science room open for those interested in experimenting and building models. I made the most of it with Jayan, a Malayalam-medium student who had a knack for building beautiful working models, though he never scored high in exams. David Sir entrusted us with the key to stay back at night in the science room to continue our experiments.

One such night, we worked well past midnight, trying to complete our models to be presented at the next day's science fair. Jayan had completed his working model of a rice mill. I had taken on an ambitious project of building an electric motor using an empty spool of thread mounted on a pencil sharpened at both ends. I wound the spool with wires which should have generated an electromagnetic field that should cause it to spin within another magnetic field. But even after giving all the connections, it stayed immobile.

"Maybe the strength of the current is insufficient," Jayan suggested. We increased the output to 24 volts, the maximum output on the adapter, but the spool was just as adamant and refused to spin.

"We will try connecting it directly to the mains," I said, ignoring his skeptical look. "The worst thing that can happen is the motor's coil getting burned up." We made the connections and put on the switch. A muffled explosion from the building's upper floor plunged us into darkness. It is in such crucial situations that being a smoker has its advantages. Jayan had a box of matches with him. As we made our way outside, we saw the lights had gone out everywhere. We spread some old newspapers and stretched down on the floor with nothing else to do.

The sun was streaming in through the open door when we woke up. We checked around and found no power supply anywhere in the building.

"It must be the main fuse. I could have tied it up with fuse wire, but that is inside the locked office room. We will tell Newton and suffer his scolding." Jayan put up a brave face. We got on our cycles and pedaled to David Sir's house.

"That was a ridiculous thing to do. But don't worry. It could only be the fuse," he said, smiling.

At home, there was a time when we didn't have a helper, so I did the additional chores of washing clothes and milking the cow and goat while my brother helped in the kitchen

Washing clothes was a cumbersome and tedious job. The cassocks of my father would be very heavy when soaked with water, and it was backbreaking work, beating it on the washing stone. When David Sir became an entrepreneur and launched his washing machine, Daviwash, we purchased one to ease the workload. It worked differently from the usual washing machines. You had to wrap the clothes on a piston which beat up and down inside a large drum. It proved unwieldy, and we reverted to the traditional method and used the machine's drum to store rice.

The techniques for milking the cow and the goat were different. Drawing milk from the goat, which had two large teats (as opposed to the cow, with four small ones), required holding the thumb and forefinger together and pinching the top of the teat where it meets the bulge of the udder to prevent the milk from flowing back, and squeezing with the rest of the fingers to work the milk out. Milking the cow was by pinching the upper end of the teats with the thumb and forefinger and drawing it down the length of the teat.

I learned more life skills when I joined the Scouts in school and became an active member. MK was the troop leader, and I was the second leader and head of the Tiger Patrol. We learned many practical skills like tying various knots, cooking, lighting a fire, messaging in Morse code or flag signaling, finding directions with or without a compass, determining the wind's direction, etc.

We took part in the District Scout Jamboree, a ten-day camp of the scout troops of all schools in the district. Most in our battalion were Tenderfoot Scouts, the entry-level grade, with just a few Second-class Scouts, including MK and me. Most other troops had higher-ranked scouts, and we looked at their first-class and President Scout badges with envy. However, after several competitions in various skills, our troop won the championship trophy.

"You have such talented guys in your troop," the Chief Commissioner of the State said while handing over our trophy. "But why is it that none of you have gone beyond second-class? Tell your Scoutmaster to enroll you for further tests. I see at least a dozen potential President Scouts among you!"

We prepared well and approached our Scoutmaster to conduct First-Class Scouts and President Scouts tests. Still, despite our persistent pestering, he didn't take any initiative. We learned later that being a Second-Class Scout himself, he would have to bring in a Scoutmaster from another school for the tests, for which he was not very keen. Meanwhile, Kochettan had become a President Scout from his school in our village in Mallassery. He traveled to Delhi and received the award from the President of India at a glittering function.

Many of the skills gained in Scouts proved beneficial later. MK and I would communicate in Morse code when we had to share secrets, much to the chagrin of others. We would assess the wind direction while clandestinely smoking cigarettes to ensure the smell doesn't reach undesired targets. Tying an appropriate knot according to the need was a boon at all times, and during my wedding several years later, many were impressed when I tied the stipulated reef knot in record time. Knowing how to light a fire and cook various dishes came in handy after the marriage.

14. A Costly Trip Home

Basketball excited me the most of all the games we had in school, and I had a natural advantage in this game because of my height. Ten of us got selected to receive coaching, and I set my alarm to 4:30 AM each morning to reach the court by five when the warm-ups started.

The inter-school championships were due, and I was on the Junior team for players aged between ten and fourteen. There were only two teams in the junior category, so we straightway went into the finals. It was a closely fought match, and I towered above the rest of the players and repeatedly scored, leading our team to victory.

Soon as the match ended, the opposing team protested, with the match officials alleging that I was over fourteen and could have played only in the Senior category. There were loud arguments, and they declared us winners after our team manager gave in writing that he would produce proof of my age, failing which we would return the trophy. We returned to school on a bus, holding the shining cup out the window for everyone to see and shouting victory slogans. We made sure that all along the route became aware of our win.

The next time I visited Valiammachi in Mallassery, I had promised my mother that I would return within three days. I went on a trek with my cousins, climbing a rock near our house to see the spectacular view from the top. We could see Pathanamthitta town in the distance and identify some landmarks.

Climbing down, Kochettan went ahead with the others, leaving Sabuchettan and me behind. Being tired after the climb, we strolled along, and soon, those in front were not visible. We were a bit confused when we came to a fork on the trail, but we both felt we had to turn right, so we forged ahead along the path.

We knew we were lost when we reached nowhere, even after trekking for over an hour. It was getting dark, and there were no houses to be seen amidst the endless stretches of rubber trees. A man we met on the way was clueless when we told him our home address but led us to a proper road, which he said would lead to Konni, a town nine kilometers away from home. We reckoned that we would head home if we took the opposite direction. After walking for another hour, we came across our uncles and cousins who had set out searching for us, and we reached home just in time for dinner.

After three days, I was very reluctant to return but knew I would not be allowed further visits if I did not keep my word. Reaching Kozhencherry, where I had to change buses, I got into a bus heading for Thiruvalla and relaxed in the rear seat. The conductor came to issue tickets before the bus started. Reaching into the shirt pocket for the cash, my hand went down and came out at the bottom. The shirt had been slit across at the pocket; I'd been robbed!

"Sorry, I can't take you on the bus without a ticket," the conductor said. "Try reporting to the station master."

The fare to Thiruvalla was just fifty paise, but the station master was unsympathetic. "Go report at the police station," he said. "They might help you get home."

I was reluctant to approach the police, uncertain how they would behave. I toyed with the idea of walking the entire distance, but it was about twenty kilometers and might take several hours. It was then that I spotted a taxi car parked by the roadside. I gave the driver my address, got in, and relaxed while he drove me home. Appachen gaped wide-eyed as he saw me getting out of the taxi. "Please pay for the taxi. I will explain everything," I said as I walked into the house.

I passed the SSLC examination with good marks- enough to comfortably get admission to the second group for the pre-degree course in college. In those days, school life ended with the 10th standard, and we joined college for the pre-degree course. The second group comprising the science subjects, including biology, was the most sought-after one, as it was required to be eligible for admission to medical college.

Becoming a doctor was the ambition of every student and parent. Only after all the seats for the second group got filled up did people opt for the first group with mathematics and science subjects, without biology. This group was supposed to be for aspiring engineers. The third and fourth groups were arts subjects and opted for by students who couldn't get admitted to the other two. Many considered these students inferior, who could hope for only becoming teachers, clerks, or other lesser jobs. People were unaware of lucrative options like company secretaries, chartered accountants, or lawyers, and IT was unheard of.

College meant more freedom, and talking to the opposite sex was no longer taboo. Some girls in my class had been my classmates in school for several years, and we got to talk for the first time. The conversation started with an introduction like "Hi, I am Thomas" and a formal response like "I am Prameela." It didn't matter that we were together in the same class at school for over five years.

The teachers were so diverse in their attitudes, attire, and capabilities. The English department itself had a wide variety of teachers. There was George Sir who taught Shakespeare, and held the class spellbound with his eloquence and dramatic presentation. But then there was Jacob Sir, who taught grammar but could not speak a single English sentence without gross grammatical mistakes. *How did he become a professor of English?* Then there was Philip Sir, a very pious gentleman, his primary interest being the 'Students' Christian Movement.'

He tried to get his students interested in spirituality. He had little control in class, and the din in the classroom during his periods would put any fish market to shame. Then there was Cherian Sir, who was a staunch atheist. Philip Sir and Cherian Sir were always the best of friends. Most other teachers also had their quirks.

Anna Kochamma was an English lecturer whose lectures also could barely be heard above the din of the class. She had a significant squint which made it difficult for us to figure out which way she was looking, so we often got pulled up for pranks which we thought were away from her field of vision. Whenever she asked a question, she sounded out Aju to answer. We were confused as we didn't have anyone by that name in class but later realized it was Cleetus, her nephew in our batch. Aju was his pet name at home. I liked the name so much that I gave this name to my firstborn years later.

I used the increased freedom to the utmost. We cut classes and spent time in a cafeteria behind the college, where like-minded students played cards, smoked cigarettes, and engaged in serious political discussions.

15. 'Born Again'

Life took a dramatic turn when I got under the influence of a spiritual group in college. The person most responsible for this change was a classmate, P. T. Mathew. He had been an inmate of a Christian Ashram in a remote village in North India. The inmates of the Ashram remained unmarried and led a celibate life.

Born to poor parents, he had been 'gifted' to the Ashram as soon as he finished school, and he spent five years there involved in their work. The Ashram authorities realized he was a bright and intelligent boy and sent him to our college for further studies. The plan was to sponsor him to study medicine at Vellore Medical College after finishing his pre-degree to use his services in the Ashram as a doctor.

Being much older than the rest of the students and being very spiritual, the other students and the teachers treated him with respect. The church had arranged accommodation for him at the Bible Institute, of which my father was the Principal. Thus, we lived on the same campus and often traveled to college together. Under his influence, I came to accept Jesus as my 'Lord and Saviour' and was officially declared 'born again,' whatever that meant.

I gave up smoking and bunking classes and read the Bible regularly. Not much further changes were needed since I was not used to lying, thieving, or murder. In a meeting, they brought one such person, a murderer who was born again while in jail and got an early release for good behavior. He had a tremendous impact, and a couple of new students got born again after hearing his testimony.

I sounded comparatively bland when giving a testimony since I had nothing dramatic to narrate. "Have more punch in your confession," George Cherian, a leader in our group, told me. I had heard him many times when he gave his testimony. He was so impressive, lifting his arms with his eyes raised to heaven, sometimes kneeling, his voice breaking and tears streaming down his face as he related his past sinful life.

My dissolution with my new life started one day in the examination hall. George Cherian was sitting a few rows in front of me, and I could clearly see him copying from a cheat sheet he was holding under the desk in his left hand.

I also resented how P. T. Mathew seemed to control every aspect of my life, like how I dressed, how long my sideburns were, and how wide my bell-bottoms should be. My father had never interfered in such matters.

I attended a Christian boy's camp that was much more liberal and progressive with its ideologies. There was a sex counselor who gave frank and open insights and systematically demolished the sinful picture of masturbation implanted in me.

"It is a universal phenomenon indulged in by all individuals at least at some point in their lives- right from the holy Pope to the lowly pauper, in some form or other," he said. "It is a healthy release of sexual urges and frustrations." His words liberated me from the immense feelings of guilt that I harbored.

The camp had study groups that discussed the Bible and its teachings, and we were free to ask questions and argue. One speaker elaborated on the power of faith and how an iota of faith could move mountains. He quoted from the Bible what Jesus is supposed to have said- "For truly I say to you, if you have faith the size of a mustard seed, you will say to this mountain, 'Move from here to there,' and it will move, and nothing will be impossible to you."

I was skeptical about this, so I raised my hand to ask a question. "Sir, are you a believer and have faith in God?"

"Of course," he replied.

"So could you please move that adjacent building just a few feet this side?"

The entire group burst into laughter. "It is also written, 'Thou shalt not make trial of the Lord, thy God,'" he said to wriggle out from the situation.

Before dinner, an hour was allotted for a discussion on the 'Problem of the Homeless.' There was an activist lawyer, Adv. Alex who was doing a lot of good work trying to rehabilitate them. He described the problem as having enormous proportions, and building homes for them would require massive investment.

I knew he was right. If I passed through Thiruvalla town at night, I could see the tramps crammed into every inch of space available on the narrow verandas in front of the shops. I used to wonder how they could withstand the chilly nights. While it rained, they would surely get wet when the wind blew.

As speaker after speaker elaborated on this hopeless problem, I felt a sudden flash of an idea and rushed forward to reveal my brilliant solution when they opened the floor for discussion.

"We can easily solve this problem if the church's authorities are willing," I suggested enthusiastically. "We have churches throughout the country, and we use them mostly only on Sundays. They are lying idle at night. Why can't we open these churches for the homeless to spend their nights?"

Most greeted my suggestion with laughter, but some were angry with the idea, which they deemed as desecrating the church. As we dispersed for dinner, a senior bishop called me to him. "You are the son of one of our priests? Tell him first to open up the Bible Institute he is in charge of!"

"But Thirumeni, he will need your permission to do that."

"Really? Tell him to apply for permission if he dares!" So saying, the bishop caught my stomach as if in a friendly gesture and gave me a hard squeeze. I was sure he meant it to hurt- which was not fair, as I couldn't (shouldn't) hit him back.

Adv. Alex came and sat next to me as we were having dinner. "I appreciate the sincerity in your suggestion," he said. "But it won't work out. Nobody will agree to open up our churches for them. But I see in you a future. Commit your life to social upliftment."

I confided in him my ambition to be a doctor.

16. Emergency

In my eagerness to study the Bible, I rummaged through my father's extensive collection of theological books, and I found most of them to be down-to-earth and rational- something I could relate to. None of them had the air of rabid spirituality espoused by the groups I had come across in college.

I learned the Bible is not a book but a collection of over 60 books written by multiple authors over three centuries and that much of what they wrote should be taken with a generous pinch of salt. William Barclay was one theologian who impressed me the most, and I became fascinated by the concept of Liberation Theology.

Around that time, an Emergency was declared by the then Prime Minister, Indira Gandhi, presumably to protect the country from going into anarchy. However, most people perceived it to be for defending herself and her authority. Dissidents and opposition leaders were arrested all over the country, and the police were given a free hand.

I found it amusing that most 'spiritual' people supported the emergency. *How could they?* People were taken by force and sterilized. They put many honest citizens behind bars for daring to speak up for democracy. But the police took care to leave most religious leaders alone, anticipating a mass uprising. One such person was the Metropolitan of our church.

I witnessed the proceedings of the 'Sabha Mandalam,' the supreme church assembly that decided on the church's policies, taking a pass to the visitor's gallery. The main agenda was to unify our church with two other churches to make it a pan-India denomination. The other two churches were formed primarily from new converts to Christianity by foreign missionaries, including many from the lower castes.

The house was divided on the issue, with the majority opposing the unification, citing the uniqueness of our church which had its history tracing back two thousand years to St. Thomas, the disciple of Jesus Christ, who came to India and gave a start to the churches here. They dropped the idea. I realized that pride and caste issues were relevant even among Christian believers who boast of not having such prejudices.

The Metropolitan, in his presidential address, spoke against the Emergency and how it was against the basic principles of democracy. I could see senior priests looking at each other and shaking their heads, shocked at Thirumeni's indiscretion. No one spoke to support his views, and ultimately, everyone ignored his remarks. Though many had similar sentiments, none were bold enough to speak up like him, fearing the repercussions. The assembly also turned down his appeals to consider the unification with the other churches.

Later, there were rumors that Indira Gandhi had ordered his arrest for speaking against the Emergency. Still, the state's Chief Minister persuaded her to desist from it, suggesting that it would be best to ignore his words. Arresting the Metropolitan might lead to an uprising that could be difficult to control.

Next Sunday, I listened with rapt attention as my father delivered his weekly sermon from the church's pulpit. He had chosen a unique subject for that day- 'The virtues of disobedience.' To drive home the point, he narrated the story of 'The boy who stood on the burning deck' - the same story that my grandfather told me several years ago. But the moral given to the story was just the opposite this time. Nobody missed the relevance of that sermon to the prevailing political atmosphere.

The final exams of the pre-degree course were over, and I waited for the results. I had scored good marks in my first year, and if I was close enough this year, I could join Medicine. When the results came, the average percentage of my marks had gone down drastically! I found it hard to believe. I was feeling quite satisfied with my performance in the exams. Now, my medical entrance was in serious doubt.

Going through the detailed mark list, I could not get over the feeling that there had been some error. I had always stood first in college in English, but the mark list showed that I had barely passed the subject in the second year. My parents, who were very disappointed with my marks, felt the same when I pointed out this discrepancy. We decided to apply for a revaluation.

Traveling to Trivandrum, our state's capital city, we reached the office of the University of Kerala. It was an imposing edifice, and we must have walked several miles within the building, going from one department to another.

"It is quite natural for students to feel that they have not received their deserved marks," an official advised my father. "It is a universal phenomenon. And if you apply for revaluation in all the subjects, it will cost you a significant sum."

Another official was a bit more sympathetic. "Since you feel there has been a mix-up while compiling your marks, it might be better to go for a recounting. It costs significantly less, and you will get to know the outcome much earlier."

We decided on recounting and got all the forms, but our money would not be sufficient. Since they based medical admission on the marks for the science subjects, we applied for recounting for only those subjects and went to pay for it at the counter, only to find that it was already closed for the day. The next day was a holiday, followed by a Sunday. We decided I would come alone later with enough cash to apply for all subjects.

Tired and dejected when we reached home late at night, I perked up seeing a letter from Vellore Medical College. It had been delivered in the morning, just after we left. I had cleared the entrance test and was chosen for the interview!

There were sixty seats available, for which they invited 120 candidates, so there was a fifty-fifty chance. The date was just one week away. If selected, I should stay back till I finish the first year, so I had to carry all I would need for that time. We put off the visit to the University to apply for the recounting and started preparations for the trip to Vellore.

17. Vellore Medical College

My mother recalled that her cousin, Babuchayan, was working at Vellore Medical College as a lecturer in Ophthalmology and suggested we contact him for guidance. Appachen straightaway rejected the idea, pointing out the relevant paragraph in the prospectus forbidding contact with any college staff and that it would lead to immediate disqualification.

Mom was crying when they bid me farewell at the railway station. P. T. Mathew accompanied me, we being the only two people who got the invitation for the interview from our college. We had sponsorship from the church, as most others had, but were not selected for the interview. *Was there a criterion by which we got a more robust backing?*

We both carried the heavy baggage with everything needed for a one-year stay. They put us up at different hostels, and we did not see each other again throughout the interview. I found we were the only two candidates who had come alone- all the others had at least one parent accompanying them.

The interview was a three-day affair and had various skill tests, personality tests, GK tests, and group discussions. I did very well in all of them. As part of the personality test, we had a questionnaire to fill up, in which one question was- 'Who do you like more? Father/Mother.' There were only two options. It was a tough choice. I pondered over this for some time before ticking 'Father.' He was the person who always let me try new things and gave us the freedom to explore.

One interviewer asked me about this answer. "It is unusual for a boy to answer like this. Do you have any homosexual orientation?" I was taken aback, and he did not seem convinced when I insisted I was not gay.

The next interviewer asked me why I wanted to be a doctor. I answered that I've always had this desire, and I wanted to serve in a village with no medical facilities. He did not hide his disbelief as he smirked and moved on to the next question. Maybe most candidates gave a similar answer.

It was a spirited discussion during the debating session. Even from the beginning, I had noticed firm support for the Emergency and Indira Gandhi by all in Vellore Medical College. That the Prime Minister had supported the college for its exclusive rights in student admissions against new rules by the state government, which tried to bring in their criteria, might have influenced their attitude.

The topic was 'Compulsory Sterilization.' I found myself pitted against all the other candidates who argued in favor. It was one against twelve, or rather one against fifteen, as I discovered that the three staff members evaluating the discussions favored compulsory sterilization. I became exhausted after defending against all the others. That night, sleep eluded me. More than the prospect of gaining admission there, I could not fathom how so many people seem to be supporting the draconian methods of the government in a democratic nation like ours.

The medical fitness examination was on the last day of the interview. After drawing my blood and taking a urine sample for routine tests, they took us to a room and asked us to strip completely. While thus standing fully naked, a junior doctor took his time examining me and filling out various forms. Two girls in white overcoats came in casually and talked to each other in whispers giggling and looking unashamedly at my nakedness. I felt sure they pre-arranged it as a sort of pre-admission ragging.

They put up the results at night on the third day. I was not on the list, and neither was P. T. Mathew. I was disappointed in myself and could not imagine why P. T. Matthew, sponsored by the Ashram for getting a doctor to work in a village in North India, was rejected.

I went to meet Babuchayan at his quarters within the campus. "I didn't come to meet you earlier, as they specified in the interview intimation letter that meeting any staff member would automatically disqualify me."

"That's bullshit!" he was livid. "They do get influenced, but I, as a junior lecturer, don't have any voice." He handed me the cup of tea his wife, a microbiologist in the same college, brought in. "So what next?" he asked me after expressing his sympathies.

He listened as I informed him of my firm resolve to be a doctor, even if it meant completing my BSc or post-graduation. He thought for a while before responding.

"But all that will take five years! Is it really worth it?"

On the way back on the train, I asked P. T. Mathew how it could be that he could not make it. "It is the ashram people themselves who scuttled my chance. They asked me for a written undertaking agreeing to become a permanent inmate of the Ashram by not marrying and leading a celibate life and, if selected, to work with them as a doctor there for the rest of my life. I agreed to the latter, but I had not decided on a monkish life. After being here in this mixed college and interacting with both sexes, I felt I would prefer to marry and have a family life. They were not willing for that, and it seems they have informed the college authorities of their disinterest in my selection."

Back home, with the option of pursuing medical studies in Vellore out of reckoning, I remembered about applying for the recounting of my marks. I left the next day for Trivandrum with the forms and money. On reaching the University office, I learned that the last day for the application was just the day before.

I turned to books to get my mind away from the depression and waited to see my chances of admission to government medical colleges. But when that came, I had missed by a whisker. Had I scored just two marks more, I could have gotten it. I could join dentistry, agriculture, veterinary sciences, or ayurvedic medicine, but I had made up my mind. It must be Modern Medicine!

Three of my friends, including MK and Cleetus, were successful, and they all started preparations to join Trivandrum Medical College.

With three-fourths of the seats reserved for graduates, there was a good chance if I tried again after I did a science degree for three years. I decided to go for it and joined BSc in Zoology. All my friends and relatives advised me against this decision. 'You should join for dentistry or agriculture, which are equally good career options.' But my father supported my decision. "Aim for what you want in life."

I spent my time languishing at home with books for company. One day, the supreme head of our church, His Holiness, Alexander Mar Thimothios, visited our home. He was related to my grandmother and dropped by to inquire about her health from my mother. Seeing me, he asked about my studies. My father informed him that I failed to get admission both in Vellore and Government Medical College and of my decision to join for BSc and try Medicine again.

"You mean to say he was selected for the interview in Vellore? Why didn't you tell me then?"

"Yes," my father confirmed. "But why should I have told you this?"

Thirumeni seemed aghast at hearing my father's reply. "Aren't you a priest in our church? And am I not related to your wife?" Thirumeni seemed disturbed, sat for some time as if thinking to say anything more, and continued. "This year, many candidates were selected for the interview from our church, and they informed us that they can select only one candidate from our denomination. Another denomination, The Christian Army, had complained to them that none of their candidates had been selected in the last few years and demanded at least three seats. A member from my former parish, who was close to me from a long time back while I was still a young priest, informed me that his son was attending the interview and to please help in whatever way possible. I put in a word for him, and he was selected."

He paused to look at me and quickly shifted his gaze back to Appachen. "Would I have done that if you had told me?" he asked in an accusing voice. "I certainly would have recommended your son!"

Why do they go through this three-day selection process if this is the way they select students? I did not express the doubts and anger flashing within me.

18. Unborn Again!

Having narrowly missed Medical College, getting admission to BSc was a cakewalk, and I was on top of the admission list. P. T. Mathew left the Ashram and enrolled as a Theology student in a Christian Seminary.

Life as a zoology student was an easy-going affair. I was unborn from my 'Born Again' status and reverted to my old habits. I started smoking again and spent most of the time outside, in a coffee shop behind the college. I didn't find the syllabus very challenging. Even without attending class, I could come first in all the internal exams, and I turned to other things. They elected me the class representative.

Zoology class mainly consisted of girls. There were just seven males to thirty-two females in my class. We were a close-knit group and thick friends who could talk about anything, even between sexes.

Some teachers were not so happy with the closeness between different genders. George Sir, a puritan to the core, was one such person.

As some of us- male and female, were talking and laughing with abandon on the steps leading to our department, he walked solemnly towards us, spoke just one sentence- "Remember this is a holy place," and walked back. We stared after him with wide eyes and open mouths. As soon as he had disappeared, we burst out into guffaws. None of us could figure out what unholy act we had engaged in.

I took my role as class representative seriously. So when I saw Sonu was absent that day, I made inquiries from other students near his house. Sonu was a diligent student who never missed a single class. We heard that his father had passed away, which was why he was absent.

Sonu's father was familiar, and we had met many times when he visited the college. We decided to pay our respects. We pooled some cash to buy a good wreath and set off to his house, about ten kilometers away. We had to board two buses to reach the place and saw the house locked. Intrigued, we walked around. Seeing the wreath in my hands, some neighbors directed us to another house about a hundred meters away, saying, "The body is kept there."

As we approached, we were relieved to see the unmistakable signs of death. There was a makeshift pavilion for the grievers and a black flag tied to the coconut tree in front. We made our way into the house through the crowd, me leading the way with the wreath in my hands. I abruptly halted in my tracks, seeing Sonu's father standing in the doorway!

"That is Sonu's father standing there!" I whispered to Rajan, who was just behind me.

"How can that be? Did he not die?" He asked, baffled. "Who died then?"

We stood there, not knowing what to do next. Sonu's father came to me. "Come! Come inside." We went in, and I solemnly placed the wreath on the dead body draped in white. We folded our hands and bowed low before beating a hasty retreat. "Who was it?" we continued to wonder.

"I never expected you all to come and pay respects when my father's uncle died," Sonu told us when he came to class the next day. "Even my father was wondering why you should have bothered." We all had a hearty laugh.

On a hot summer day, Jesus Christ came to visit my father. He was the sexton of our home church at Mallassery, responsible for maintaining the church and premises and assisting the vicar during church service. He was nicknamed 'Jesus Christ' because he was the only person who could bring to life the antique clock adorning the church's front wall, each Sunday. He had come with a specific purpose. "Please talk to my son and try to reform him. He has gone wayward. Shall I send him to you so you can talk some sense into him?"

My father looked at him, surprised. Jesus Christ's son was a notorious drunkard for years, always getting into trouble. "What has he done now?" he asked.

"I feel ashamed to even talk about it," Jesus Christ lamented. "He has left our church to join a Pentecostal group!"

"But what about his drunkenness?" my father inquired. "Those joining these Pentecost churches usually give up drinking."

"Oh, he has stopped all that, but how do I face anyone now? He has brought disgrace to our whole family."

Appachen gave him a piece of his mind and sent him off with a stern message not to bother which church he goes to but to be thankful that he had given up drinking.

At church service next Sunday, my father chose to speak about the proper upbringing of children. He related this incident without naming Jesus Christ and observed that children are the product of their parents, not only in the biological aspect.

He spiced it up with a short story about a jeweler who specialized in repairing antique clocks. A customer once came to him carrying the pendulum of a clock and complained that it did not oscillate now. The watchmaker sent him back, telling him to keep the pendulum and bring the clock, which needed repairs.

In my second year of BSc, my grandfather, bedridden for years, became unconscious and remained in a coma. I went to see him just when the doctor arrived, and there was just grandma, the helpers, and me when he came. He did a quick examination and prescribed some medicines and injections. "I will arrange for my apothecary to come and give the injections. His situation is critical. Please inform everyone, in case."

"Shouldn't we have paid the doctor?" I asked Grandma when he left.

"I don't know," she replied. "But when my children come, they will settle everything."

My uncles started arriving one by one. Kunjachen Uncle, who lived in Kuwait, was the first to arrive. "Please hire a taxi for me," he asked me. "We will see the doctor at his clinic."

A sizeable crowd was waiting at the doctor's office when we arrived, but he called us inside when the pharmacist informed him of our arrival. "He's had a massive cerebral hemorrhage. There is nothing much to be done. He will live for just two or three days more," he informed us in an ominous tone.

Uncle nodded, stood up, and took a hundred rupee note from his purse. "Thank you so much, Doctor," he said in a broken voice as he handed the cash to the doctor. He turned and left, with me following him wide-eyed, more out of seeing a hundred rupee note for the first time.

Grandpa died just two days later. The halo over the doctor's head shone brighter in my mind.

19. A Mysterious Light from the Grave

Kunjachen Uncle arranged for his funeral the next day, by which time all his brothers would arrive, except for Bombay Uncle could reach only the day after, and he didn't want to risk Grandpa's remains decomposing before the last rites. He persuaded the church authorities to agree that they would lower the casket into the pit with the lid closed after the funeral service and not cover it with earth. When Bombay Uncle came, they could remove it for him to see Grandpas's face and pay his last respects. The arrangements amused me. *Why is it so important to see a dead man's face? Isn't it better to remember his face as it was when he was alive?*

"Keeping the body safe throughout the night will be your responsibility," the Vicar said sternly. "Keep a watchman to guard the body." There was merit in his words. My grandpa had two or three gold fillings in his teeth, and they did not remove his gold wedding ring while burying him. *Why don't they remove it? What good will it do for anyone if it gets buried forever? It might get into the hands of graveyard thieves!*

"But who will be willing to spend the night in the cemetery?" George Uncle asked the Vicar.

"There is a member of the church committee who can arrange someone. You can pay him the cost, and he will organize things."

The member asked and received fifteen rupees for the service. "Wait here till the watchman arrives," he advised. We all waited at the cemetery. The watchman came at five o'clock in the evening, and he seemed to be quite drunk. "Anybody will touch the body only over my dead body," he declared and took over, and we left for home.

Huddled in chairs in the courtyard, my uncles sat talking, sharing Grandpa's memories and discussing the arrangements for the complete burial once Bombay Uncle reached.

"Is that man trustworthy? Let us check on him. That drunken guy didn't seem at all reliable." Kunjachen Uncle was anxious. "After dinner, we will walk to the cemetery and make sure he is doing his job."

All of us set out after our dinner of rice gruel with lentils. George Uncle was visibly nervous about going to the cemetery. Still, he trudged along, fortified by the company of five other people accompanying him, including yours truly, the only one from the next generation.

We reached the gate of the burial ground but couldn't see the watchman anywhere. An intermittent rumbling sound arose from inside the grave where Grandpa lay. Fascinated, I noticed a strange glow shining from inside the pit. Looking back at the group, I saw they had stopped in their tracks. George Uncle looked panic-stricken and turned around as if preparing to make a run for it.

Given my prior experience with graveyards, I was not panicky but still intrigued. The glow inside the grave was not the same greenish-yellow flame I've seen in cemeteries caused by burning phosphorus, and the intermittent rumbling sound was a pure mystery. Armed with a torchlight, I made for the grave, shining my torch on the ground ahead. I stopped in my tracks as I saw a snake slithering across. "Snake!" I shouted.

"Come back!" George Uncle called. "We'll come after daylight to see things. We don't want another tragedy now."

"Let me see what it is!" I shouted back as I made my way forward and shone my torchlight down into the grave. My eyes had never set sight upon a weirder scene. Lying over the closed casket, our watchman snored away, deep in sleep. A lighted kerosene lamp kept by his side gave out a golden-yellow radiance. A long dagger with a shiny blade lay glittering by his side.

"Are you sleeping on the job?" I shouted, trying to wake him.

His response was sharp. "Who is it?" he screamed as he sprang onto his feet, wielding the long dagger pointed toward me. I jumped back to a safe distance. "It's me! Grandpa's grandson!" I gasped, quickly revealing my identity lest he attacked.

"You! What are you doing here?" I was relieved to see him strapping the dagger back to his waist before climbing up from the grave.

"We came to check on you," I said, regaining my composure and trying to sound stern. "The others are there at the gate." I led him to the cemetery entrance, shining my torch on the ground and taking heavy steps so that any snake on the way would keep away.

"Is this how you keep guard?" John Uncle asked angrily.

"What better way, Sir?" the watchman argued. "Anyone can get to the corpse only over my dead body!" Nobody could find fault with his logic.

Bombay Uncle arrived early the next day, and we made our way again to the cemetery. The night's watchman was waiting for us. He removed the coffin cover for uncle to see Grandpa one last time. I peeked in too. The flowers over the body had wilted, and Grandpa's face looked puffed up. Climbing back into the grave, the watchman replaced the lid over the coffin. He then heaped earth into the pit covering the coffin, and Grandpa was left buried forever.

We thanked the watchman for his services. "You gave us a real scare yesterday," remarked John Uncle, giving him an extra tip.

Soon, my uncles left for their homes abroad, and Grandma was left alone in the house with a maid. My mother and I took turns to visit and check up on her.

20. College Elections During Emergency

While engrossed in a novel one day, Appachen called me. "Coming with me to see Mother Teresa? She is coming to visit our orphanage."

I'd heard about this nun doing a lot of social work, and the orphanage was just a few minutes' walk from my house, but I was not enthused. Appachen did not press me and went alone. It was a momentary decision that I regret to this day.

The elections to the College Student Union were coming up, and it was poised to be a fierce contest between the rival camps. That year, with the Emergency prevailing, general elections were suspended. There would only be a representative type of election, with the voting done among the class representatives.

We worked out the relative strengths of the opposing camps. There were thirty-eight class representatives. The student groups supporting the Congress Party came to sixteen, and those with us, the opposition, were seventeen.

Five class representatives didn't have any known allegiance, and the rival camps launched frantic efforts to woo them over to their side. We got the support of three; one person supported the Student's Congress Union, and another remained undecided. Having the firm backing of twenty class representatives, we became confident of winning. I was the candidate from my group to contest for the post of Vice-Chairman.

The Principal called us into the classroom, which was converted into a polling station on election day. We saw that three of the class reps who supported us were absent. The process was to start, but we asked for more time.

"I cannot allow that! The schedule is fixed." Philip Sir, the Polling Officer, was firm. The polling went on, and the Students Congress won every seat by a single vote. Perplexed and sad, we went in search of those absent. We found the first person at his house.

"Why are you here? Why didn't you come to the elections?" We asked in exasperation.

"I had set out well ahead of time when a group of five thugs came in a car and stopped me. A police team followed them in a jeep. They warned me against voting and told me to stay put at home. 'You will face the consequences if you dare to go out and vote,' they threatened me."

We reached out to the next person at his home, and it was the same story. At the third house, his father was surprised to see us. "He went three hours ago, saying he was going to college to vote for the Students Union elections. Didn't you see him?"

"No, we didn't! That's why we have come."

His parents became concerned. "Please inform me if you get to know where he is," his father pleaded.

We left, promising that we sure will. As we turned the corner, we saw him coming towards the house. He looked disheveled, and we all rushed to surround him. "What happened to you? You look awful!" I exclaimed.

"I was coming to vote for the elections. A group of goondas stopped me about a hundred meters before the college gate. They seemed to have police protection; a police jeep was parked some distance away, and they were watching the action from inside. The goondas threatened me and told me not to vote, but I resisted saying it was my right. 'Seems he is not willing to listen to reason,' one of them said and commanded to his gang of thugs. 'Get him into the car!'

"They pulled me into the car, blindfolded me, then took me to a vacant house and kept me there. Just sometime back, they brought me back to near this place. Removing my blindfold, they pushed me out and threatened dire consequences if I complained. Please, let's leave it at that- my parents will be worried sick."

The next day, we visited the Principal at his office. "I understand your frustration," he admitted. "But you know the situation. What can I do? If I cancel the election and inquire, I will be the next target. I have my family to think of!"

This incident made me furious, and resentment against the Emergency obsessed me. I came in contact with an underground group that was working against it. Some radical elements advocated terrorist methods like planting bombs and derailing trains, but I quickly distanced myself from them. Whatever the cause, I found it inconceivable to put innocent lives at risk.

Near my home resided Dr. K K Thomas, a renowned theologist. He was a proponent of Liberation Theology, which was gaining acceptance among Christian youth. He was an internationally known figure and the Secretary of the World Council of Churches. That could be why they did not arrest him for his anti-Emergency activities.

A small group of like-minded people met at his house and planned activities to oppose the Emergency in whatever way possible- the focus was on spreading awareness. I was the youngest among them. We had a magazine called 'Action for Freedom,' printed and published secretly and distributed to the public by hand.

I had a cloth bag slung over my shoulders which contained my college file with notes from the classes and a few copies of the 'Action for Freedom,' which I was distributing to contacts. I had just given a copy to Jacob Sir, a professor in our college, and was walking to the house of a retired teacher to give him a copy when a police jeep pulled up straight in front, almost colliding with me.

"Get in!" The officer sitting in front commanded me, but I stood there hesitating. "Get in!" This time, he was loud and menacing. I got into the jeep, which sped away straight to the police station.

21. A Meek Revolutionary

Nobody spoke a word, and I was too scared to ask anything. They took me to a cabin inside; I read the name board in front- Jacob Thomas. Circle Inspector.

"Open that bag!" he ordered. I did as told and held it up to him. He took my college file and threw it on the table with a cursory glance. Next, he took out the small bundle of the Action for Freedom magazines. "Now, what do we have here?"

"It's just some Christian literature that we circulate," I said respectfully.

He opened one of them and started reading aloud. "Any government that tramples on individual freedom and free press does so with the ulterior motive of stifling democracy and establishing absolute power, and has to be opposed and brought down at any cost'- Now, how is this Christian literature? This is a political magazine, and you are working against the government and the Emergency."

He looked up at me and continued in a condescending tone. "Don't you know that anarchy was reigning here before the Emergency, and you want to destabilize the government, which has brought order and stability?" I gazed at him and kept mum, guilt written on my face. "Have you received training to make bombs?"

His abrupt question jolted me to answer. "No, Sir!" I blurted out. "We don't believe in any violent means."

"Where did you get this propaganda material?" I wondered if it would be okay to tell him the truth. Indeed, they wouldn't dare pull up Dr. K K Thomas. Anyway, I just kept my mouth shut.

"I know how to make you talk, but I don't believe in violent means. Besides, you don't look healthy enough, and I don't want blood on my hands." He turned to a police officer. "Keep him in the lock-up, and take his clothes. He will talk tomorrow morning."

"Come," the police officer said, leading me to the lock-up room. His voice seemed kind. I looked at his face, and recognition dawned on me. It was Saji's father!

Saji Mathew was a good friend in college. We were in the same batch, but he was a history student. We visited each other's homes and knew the parents.

"My parents!" I whispered to him. 'They will be worried. Please ask Saji to tell them I will spend the night at a friend's place."

He nodded. "Get into the lock-up room and take off your clothes." He paused a moment. "Keep your underwear now, but you may have to remove it later if CI Sir insists."

I undressed down to my underwear and got into the room. The heavy metal door with bars closed behind me. I looked around. Another man was in the dimly lit room, sleeping on the bare floor.

He stirred awake and looked me over. "Hello! It looks like I will have company tonight. What is your name? And why are you here?"

I sat on the floor talking to him. He introduced himself as Soman. He had landed up here, caught stealing a bicycle. I noticed he had his clothes on. "Didn't they take your clothes?" I asked him.

"No, my dear boy, that is for the first-timers. I won't mind if they take it or not, and they know it. I have been to jail many times before. It's not such an awful place, you know? They give decent food. The only difficulty is the beating you get when caught to get the confession out of you. If I am foolish enough to get caught, I immediately confess to the crime, and they won't bother me much after that. But, my dear boy, you have a bright future. Why get into unnecessary trouble? Emergency or not, why should your bother? How is it going to affect you? Now be a good boy and confess to them whatever you did wrong. Beg them for mercy. They might even decide not to press charges and let you go. What they won't tolerate is defiance."

I lay down, thinking. There was practical wisdom in his advice. But how can I be such a submissive coward? On the other hand, what difference will my resistance make to the outcome? Sleep eluded me. *Will this be the end of my aspirations in life?*

The room was damp and cold, my stomach was rumbling, and I felt myself shivering. Soman noticed it too. He removed his shirt and lungi and gave them to me. "Wear the shirt and use the lungi as a bedsheet. Otherwise, you will get cold from the floor."

I hesitated before accepting his generosity. "Don't worry about me," he continued. "I am least affected by this. I have lots of experience lying here without clothes. Anyway, it is much more comfortable than my house, which has a leaky roof, and I have to search for a spot where water doesn't bother me when it rains."

I might have dozed off in between, but when they opened the bars early in the morning, I was wide awake. Saji's father handed me my clothes. "I have talked to the CI about you. Don't be clever or obstinate, and agree with whatever he says. That way, you might stay away from further trouble.

The Circle Inspector was not so harsh the next day, but he gave me a mocking look. "So, how is the young revolutionary today?" I just stood there without answering.

"Isn't it from Dr. K K Thomas that you got those pamphlets?" he asked me, looking straight into my eyes. I nodded silently.

"Mr. Varghese here told me about you. You are the son of a priest- a respected one at that. And it seems you are an excellent student in college. You have a bright future. Take my advice and keep away from unlawful activities. Don't spoil your future with immature actions."

He picked up a sheet of paper from the table, studied it intently, then tore it up and threw it into the dustbin. "I am letting you go now without registering a case, but remember, if you repeat such activities, there will be no leniency." He returned my cloth bag, minus the Action for Freedom magazines.

I walked home, relieved but in turmoil. My father was shocked to see me with bloodshot eyes and messy hair. "Why are you looking so haggard? Did you not sleep?"

"We stayed up all night to study," I lied. After a quick shower and a heavy breakfast, I felt relaxed. The grumbling in my stomach eased, and I felt sleepy. "I have a headache and am not going to college today. I want to take a rest," I said and flopped onto my bed.

In the evening, I had a messenger from Dr. K K Thomas. "We have suspended the group for the time being; many are under arrest. It seems they spared you now because you are just a student. We will not be having regular meetings in the immediate future."

22. The End of Emergency

After my encounter with the police, I lay low. In early 1977, Indira Gandhi declared elections. Maybe she felt confident about winning, considering the calm atmosphere by then. There were few agitations mainly because the opposition was in jail, and there also was a lot of international pressure.

They freed many opposition leaders with the declaration for elections, and we restarted our campaign with a vengeance. From early morning till late night, we trudged on foot from door to door, urging people to vote against Congress. I would be dead tired by evening, not having an appetite to have supper- maybe because of the many cups of tea and coffee throughout the day.

As we told the voters, this was the last chance to choose between democracy and dictatorship. We left no stone unturned in our relentless campaign. Friends noticed I had lost weight. 'You are a walking skeleton now!'

It was a Sunday, and I sat glued to the radio, listening to the election results, which had started to trickle in. By evening, Congress was losing, and Indira Gandhi lost in her constituency.

Sunil, my senior in college, whose hatred for Indira Gandhi was no secret, came running from his house a few blocks away. Not knowing how to celebrate, we started screaming at the top of our voices and jumping up and down. But this was too immense to keep to ourselves. In a two-man procession, we took to the road shouting slogans like "Long Live Democracy! Down with Indira Gandhi" and "Jai Hind!"

Amused onlookers looked out from the windows of their homes. Many rushed towards us to confirm if the news was indeed trustworthy. "We heard it ourselves on All India Radio," we assured them.

"Unbelievable!" was the most common reaction. A few joined us, and we walked along the roads and bylanes, taking a circuitous route. Soon, Sunil and I were leading a procession of scores of people.

There were sounds of fireworks from somewhere. It had become dark. I looked at my watch, which showed a quarter past nine. *Folks at home will be worried.* I nudged Sunil to show him the time, and his mouth opened wide with surprise. "Let's get home!" he said.

We both made our way out of the crowd and headed home. The procession continued, with over a hundred people by then.

The Congress won in Kerala, but no Congress supporter came out to celebrate. Atrocities of the Emergency were not as pronounced in Kerala as in the states of North India because a benign Chief Minister ruled the state, the leader of a communist faction paradoxically being part of the coalition led by the Congress.

He was a principled man who did not take advantage of the Emergency's unbridled powers. People liked the relative calm- no agitations, strikes, or lockouts during the Emergency. But I felt that people in our state thought for themselves rather than focus on the larger picture of democracy vs. dictatorship in the country.

The next day, the congressmen held a victory rally with flags and banners. They halted in front of Sunil's and my house, shouting slogans. However, their joy seemed dampened by the crushing defeat suffered at the national level.

I don't think I would have gotten involved in politics had it not been for the Emergency. The Janata Party, formed by merging all the non-communist opposition parties, came to power, and they selected me to be the district Vice-President of its student wing.

The election to the Students Union for the new year was declared. The Student's Janata put me up as the Chairman candidate. My opponent was Mathew John, who had been the Chairman the previous year, too. He was a popular figure on the campus, organizing many events and programs during his tenure. We were good friends.

The Students' Congress was still the most popular party on the campus despite the Emergency, and the election results were a foregone conclusion. Even so, it was a victory of sorts that I lost by only about fifty votes.

The evening they announced the results, the rival camps sat on either side of the lawn in the middle of the campus. Usually, the losing team does a quiet exit, but we stayed on, singing and dancing. It seemed to everyone that we were the guys who won. After darkness had set in, members of both groups started leaving one by one. Those of us still left merged into one group. We started chatting about our novel experiences during our respective campaigns. I found myself face to face with Mathew John, my opponent.

"Why don't we have a drink together?" he asked. I was willing. Leaving our supporters, we walked away together to the toddy shop in a secluded spot at the edge of a paddy field next to the college campus. "Great fight you gave me, Thomas. I got scared in between, thinking I might lose," Mathew John told me.

"You were never in any danger of that," I responded. "I could never match your debating skills. My Malayalam is flawed, and I was hesitant about speaking in public."

"I know how you could have won this election. Tell me, why didn't you speak in English?"

"But would anyone accept it? What would they have thought about me not speaking in our mother tongue?"

Mathew gulped down the rest of the toddy, folded his hands as in prayer, and looked up to the roof. "Thank you, God, for making Thomas feel like that." Then he shifted his attention away from God and turned to me. "My dear Thomas, if you had spoken in English, I would have been a goner. You are so ignorant about the psychology of us college students. They would have been so impressed, you know? They look up to people who can speak English.

"But you should have given me this advice earlier!"

"Do you think I would and dig my own grave? As it is, you gave me a proper fight. You should contest next year. You are sure to win."

The toddy affected us, and we walked back to the college campus. We were swaying a little, steadying each other with our arms around the other's shoulders.

After the election, I came to be called Chairman. Someone who wanted to mock me might have used it derisively, but later, my friends continued to address me by this title. Even when Mathew John was with me, if someone called out "Hey Chairman!', we both turned around to see that it was me they were addressing. "I won the election, but you have become the Chairman," he would remark wryly.

College life was enjoyable. Classes were boring, so I just skipped them. I was confident about studying myself, except for that one paper in my second language, Hindi. What practical knowledge of the lingo I had gained from my stay in Bombay was useless. I remembered how it had gotten me into trouble at school when the teacher asked me the Hindi word for fish. But attending the Hindi classes was even greater torture, so I skipped that too.

It was the year-end public exam for the Hindi second paper the next day, based on a textbook on the life of Rana Pratap, a Rajput king, and that was all I knew. I had not attended classes nor read the book, and reading an entire book written in Hindi was unthinkable for me.

Wandering through town after coming from college, the exam occupied my mind. While gazing through the comic books displayed in front of a bookstore, a particular book caught my eye. It was an illustrated English comic book for children titled 'Rana Pratap!' I dashed to the bus stand, begged a friend waiting for the bus to lend me two rupees, and rushed back to buy it.

I got home late, and my father asked me why I had taken so long. "The buses were crowded, and I had difficulty getting into one," I replied.

"But didn't you take the cycle to college today?" he asked, surprised. I realized with a start that he was indeed right, and I had left my cycle in college. I grabbed a torch and ran back to the college campus. My bike was safe under the staircase, where I had kept it. I rode back home at full speed and reached just after all of them had finished dinner.

I finished supper quickly and stayed up all night going through the comic several times, memorizing all the names, dates, and details of his battles. I gained a thorough knowledge of his life. The next day in the exam, I wrote detailed answers to all the questions in whatever Hindi I could muster. When they published the exam results, I had just scraped through.

23. A Piece of Fried Banana

The NCC was a student cadre of the armed forces, having the motto, 'Unity and Discipline.' I enrolled in it with some friends, and we pledged to be responsible citizens and uphold the unity of India. It was a strenuous affair, with drills, marching in heavy uniform and boots in the scorching sun. The training became interesting, though it differed from the Scouts in school.

Koshy Sir, our professor in physics, was the NCC officer. Rifle training was exciting. One day, my target blew off from the wooden stump to which it was fixed. "Don't worry," he said, "aim for that stump. You should split it with your bullet. I will give you a special gift if you do it." Taking careful aim, I hit it, splitting the wooden pole.

He rewarded me with a go on the machine gun. The officers rarely gave students the machine gun as there was only one, and giving it to all the cadets, showing them how to operate it, was cumbersome. Since it was mandatory to use it, they would usually fire it on the hillside to flatten the earth where needed.

The feel of absolute power with my finger on the trigger and the gun going rat-a-tat at continuous high speed was incredible. I imagined myself mowing down a large crowd of attackers with its rapid fire.

Koshy Sir was happy with my overall performance in the NCC. "Next year, I want you to be the Under Officer," he declared. Fate willed otherwise. It appeared as a piece of fried banana.

Famished after the heavy drill, I went to the canteen but had just enough cash with me for a cup of tea. Mathew John and a group were having tea and munching on fried bananas. "Don't the NCC provide any refreshment after your drill?" he asked. "Quit the NCC and join us."

He referred to the NSS (National Service Scheme), a separate organization for students interested in social work. They cleaned the campus, dug roads, cleaned water bodies, and did other such jobs. After their work, they had refreshments of tea with snacks.

"Join, and you will get the refreshments now." Mathew John said and took me, still in my NCC uniform, to Varghese Sir, their Program Officer. "Of course, you are welcome," he said. "We'd love to have you with us." I joined them right there and had my fried banana.

The NSS turned out to be much more enjoyable. The boys and girls were from different backgrounds but enjoyed excellent camaraderie. There were jokes, laughter, and singing while we slugged with spades and machetes, though most were not accustomed to using them.

It was a far cry from the NCC with its strict discipline. But back in the NCC, they dubbed me as the guy who betrayed the nation for a piece of fried banana.

The NSS took us to the interior of villages, where we widened many roads and made them motorable. People donated their land bordering the thoroughfare, and we did the manual labor to convert it into a proper motorway.

One particular landlord, a retired army man, was not willing to donate his land, though he was the only one around who owned a car and would benefit from the widened road. He came with a rifle pointed toward us. "Touch my land, and you will pay with your life," he threatened.

We were young guys not afraid of death. We confronted him with slogans like "Death to the bourgeois mindset! Up with socialist thinking!"

Verghese Sir stepped in. "No confrontation, boys. If he doesn't want a good motorable road in front of his house, that is his problem. We won't take anyone's land by force. Complete the rest of the road. He will come round and change his mind." Reluctantly, we moved on to the next property and continued our work. We completed the road in a week. It looked expansive and beautiful, but for the jutting strip of land belonging to the army man.

Two weeks later, the guy felt bad that it was just his land obstructing the free flow of traffic through the motorway. The local people regarded him with contempt. He employed laborers at his own expense to excavate the ground and make it level with the road.

The local panchayat pitched in, and an expansive, tarred road that connected the village to the town center became real. We went to see the new road. Cars and jeeps cruised along, and we learned that soon there would be a bus service, a real boon for the villagers. The feeling of fulfillment was complete.

We went to clean a stream being choked to death by African weeds.

(There was no plastic waste those days.) We waded into the water, chest-deep at the deepest level. Collecting the weeds in baskets, we carried them on our heads to dump them onto the land in the sun. We heaped them at the base of the coconut trees that dotted the river bed; it was excellent manure.

The job got finished by the evening. We had a late lunch given to us packed in banana leaves, sitting on the bank and watching with contentment as the now clear water flowed downstream. Our legs were bleeding painlessly where the leeches bit and drank our blood to bloat and fall off when they had their fill. We removed those still on the job by rubbing salt over them.

Another great experience was thatching the worn-out, leaking roof of the dilapidated hut of a widow living there with three children. None of us knew such work, but an old villager guided us through the process. We slit the coconut fronds into two halves and wove the leaves into a mat. Meanwhile, a group climbed up to remove the crumbling roof. By the time they dismantled it, we had made enough leaf mats to thatch.

"We are tired. Let a new group climb up and lay the roof, one of them said as he wiped the sweat off his face and gulped down the fresh lime juice offered.

I folded up my *mundu* and climbed up with two others. Those below passed us the long, woven fronds, and we laid them on top, tying them to the rafters. We started from the lower border, working upwards to the top.

After hours of grueling effort, we completed the work and climbed down to view the finished roof. The roof was now neat and green. Some girls came up to congratulate us. Susan, always frank and blunt, singled me out for praise. "Great work!" she said, "but we didn't like the color of your underwear."

There was another girl, Jessy, in the NSS who, like me, had narrowly missed getting into Medical College after pre-degree and was now doing a bachelor's in chemistry. One year junior to me, she was also very active in the group and attended the annual ten-day camps. Though familiar since she joined college for her pre-degree, we became closely acquainted during our degree days, especially in the NSS camps.

Another organization we were together was the Brains Trust- an exclusive club of fifty of the best brains in college. I became the club's secretary, and we had debates, quiz competitions, mock assemblies, and such other activities. We divided ourselves into treasury and opposition benches for mock assemblies and flayed each other with vitriol. But I should admit that we never could match the acrimony and pandemonium in the actual State Legislative body.

Jessy was doomed to marry me several years later.

24. Zoology Student

Zoology dissection classes had their fun moments. We had to cut up various animals and dissect and display their interiors. Cockroaches, frogs, earthworms, and chameleons were the specimens involved, and everyone tried to overcome their natural aversion to these creatures.

The weak-hearted couldn't get to do it at first, but the thought of the year-end exams when we had to do these dissections was motivation enough. A few could not stop the mounting nausea that ended in vomiting episodes. The department would supply the frogs and chameleons, but as regards cockroaches and earthworms, we had to bring them ourselves.

Frogs were not repulsive to me, unlike many others, having good experience catching and handling them in the paddy fields at our family house in Mallassery. Valiammachi would fry them to make a tasty dish. "Excellent meat!" my mother exclaimed while gulping it down during lunch one day when she came to visit. But when she learned it was a frog, she rushed outside to vomit it.

I would help the others pith and nail the frogs onto the dissection board. Pithing was a humanitarian act you did on the frog by inserting a thick needle through the back of the head into the skull and mashing up the brain so the creature would not feel any more pain. We then fixed it on the board, like Christ was crucified at the cross, but with the legs nailed wide apart.

We then cut open the chest and abdomen, carefully dissected the blood vessels and nerves, displayed them by inserting small strips of black paper all along its course, and presented it to the examiner. I became a much sought-after person for help with these procedures. I became very popular with the girls, particularly for the regular supply of cockroaches I brought from the storeroom of our house, where they were available in plenty.

For me, remembering the scientific names of so many rare animals was a formidable challenge, and there were quite a few that we had to mug up. Necturus Maculosus was one such name of a salamander, but my classmates loved its common name, 'Mud Puppy.' They thought it suited me as a nickname, and thus I got stuck with it.

My second-year exams approached, and there were lots of study material that I had never gone through even once. I persuaded my parents to let me stay in a lodge with some friends to concentrate on our studies. Helping and motivating each other would boost our performance. After dinner, I would sit down and study once we returned to our rooms.

Rajan would straight away flop onto the bed. "I will have a nap and wake up early to study. Would you mind calling me at one a.m.?"

When I called him at the scheduled time, he mumbled something and turned over to continue sleeping.

"Why didn't you wake me up?" he complained in the morning. He seemed unconvinced when I told him I had tried. "You should shake me hard and somehow get me up," he said. At one o'clock the next day, the events just got repeated. I shook him, called out loudly, and tried to prop him up to a sitting position, but he would not open his eyes.

"You may use whatever method, but somehow get me up this night," he pleaded the next day. There was an ominous implication that I was not interested in getting him to study.

That night, I took drastic action. When he lay unmoving after all my efforts, I went to the bathroom, filled a bucket with water, and splashed it over him. He woke up with a start but then became furious. "Why are you so particular that I should study? Are you going to marry my sister?" He roared as he dried himself with a towel, pulled off the wet mattress, and went back to sleep on the bare bed.

I went home for the weekend and returned with plenty of snacks-banana chips, homemade *achappams* (Rose cookies), and fish pickles. Three days later, I got a message that my brother and mother had contracted chickenpox. Ten days remained before my exams, so I resolved not to visit home until it was over.

I had a headache waking up the next day, and my whole body ached. While having breakfast, Rajan noticed a blister on my neck, like a drop of water. A little later, I saw two more on my chest. The homeopathic doctor who had a clinic opposite confirmed it as chickenpox. Everyone wanted me out. "Go home at the earliest. Hope nobody has got it from you." I packed up my things and left for home. "Leave the snacks and other goodies here," Rajan advised. "We won't get Chickenpox by eating them."

I wouldn't be able to write the exams that year, and I will have to attempt both papers together the following year. But there was no choice, and I spent my time at home while my friends tackled the examinations.

I was the most affected in the family, with blisters and boils all over my body. It ached and itched all over. It was painful lying on the bed, so I stood by the window at night, holding on to its bars for support, dozing off in that position at times.

Someone suggested the leaves of the neem tree would benefit. It worked! I stroked myself with a twig full of leaves. It was so cool and soothing, and I made a paste of crushed leaves, which I applied to the boils. Spreading the leaves over the bed, I had a good night's sleep for the first time in four days.

25. A Student Politician

It was the final year in college, and events were warming up for the Students Union elections. My name came up again as a candidate for the post of Chairman, and I became tense. Pothen, the President of the Students' Janata, came to see me. "Since you came close to Mathew John last time, it will be a cakewalk for you now. This time, you will win no matter who they put up as a candidate against you."

What he said was right, but I had become disillusioned by the Janata Party. They had chosen an eighty-year-old veteran politician as the Prime Minister. I could relate to his efforts to create peace with our neighbor, but his priorities at home and dealings with foreign superpowers left much to be desired. He was chosen over many young leaders who would have been much more capable. His most important message for the world was about the benefits of drinking one's own urine. The party and government looked like a boisterous, inefficient lot.

A few friends from the SCF (Students Communist Federation) had approached me, and I was inclined to join them. Theirs was the smallest political group on the campus, having just about a score of members who were isolated by the conservative Christian atmosphere in the college. The ideals of Communism attracted me as I began studying them through books. 'Das Kapital' was too much for me, but I read simplified versions and 'The Communist Manifesto.'

I could also escape being a candidate and concentrate on my studies by exiting the party. I resigned from the Students' Janata to join the Students Communist Federation. Pothen was aghast. "You are committing political suicide as well as mutilating our party!"

I pleaded with him to understand my altered mindset and inclination. "Besides, I don't aim for a future in politics," I declared.

Robin was the President of the SCF unit in college, and he came to inform me that they had decided to contest elections with me as the Chairman candidate. I tried to plead with them to let me be, but they were insistent. My father was always tolerant and encouraged freethinking, but he tried to dissuade me. "They brainwash people with their ideology."

I objected to this. "Talking about brainwashing, haven't religious teachings brainwashed me ever since childhood? Even as a small child, I have gone to church and Sunday School. Didn't they indoctrinate me? Even if accepting the teachings of Jesus to be the ultimate truth, I feel it relates much more to Communism than any other political ideology."

"But they encourage violence! Even their flag displays the hammer and sickle- weapons to eliminate opponents. The sickle would catch the person by the neck to smash him on the head with the hammer."

"That's preposterous!" I replied. "Those symbols denote the labor class- the hammer for the industrial workers and the sickle, agricultural laborers."

My father was silent and thoughtful. I should say to his credit that he never forced me to change my decision. But my mother started crying for long periods, lamenting that her firstborn son had become a communist. One day, I was firm when I spoke to her.

"I have made my decision after considerable thought," I said. "No amount of persuasion is going to make me change my mind. This is emotional blackmail you are attempting." She never bothered me after that.

I still don't know if my father had a hand in it, but Valia Thirumeni, now the supreme head of our church, sent me an envoy requesting me to meet him in person and fix an appointment. I turned up on time and was ushered straight to his office.

Thirumeni started with pleasantries and inquired about how my studies were progressing. He still remembered my failure in getting admission into Vellore medical college, and I wondered if he realized he might have had a hand in my rejection. Getting straight to the purpose of the meeting, he looked into my eyes. "I have heard that you have joined the Communist Party?"

I confirmed with a nod of my head.

"Please tell me the reason that prompted your decision."

He listened as I explained to him how I was drawn into politics through the Janata Party because of the Emergency, how I became disillusioned, and why now I think the communist ideology is the best way forward.

Thirumeni heard me out. He nodded and said, "You know, son, I was attracted to these ideals even after becoming a priest. When I did my doctorate, I thought of preparing my thesis on Das Kapital, so I read and studied it fully. But then my interest changed, and ultimately, I earned my doctorate for my thesis on the Bhagwat Geeta."

I looked up at him with awe and respect. He smiled and continued. "You are a bright and idealistic young boy, and I don't think I should give you any advice. But doesn't Communism make you an atheist and nonbeliever?"

I replied that there had been no pressure on me, and some party members were staunch believers. Thirumeni's secretary entered to inform us that the MLA was waiting for an audience. "Okay, we will disperse with a prayer," he said and rose. While bidding me goodbye, he told me not to hesitate to contact him anytime I felt.

The following week, a group of professors from my college came home to see my father. They told him about my joining the SCF and asked him to interfere and stop my political activities in college. Appachen was candid with his response.

"He was a candidate last year, but none of you came with such a request. It seems you people are not against campus politics, but the particular political party. He is now grown up, and political affiliations are his personal decisions, and I don't want to interfere."

Though I tried to back out, the SCF fielded me as the Chairman candidate. I worried that such activities would make my studies suffer. I was in my final year and had my second-year subjects pending.

Canvassing for votes, I could feel many of my close friends in a spot, as they found it difficult to bring themselves to vote for a communist. I didn't want to make them feel too uncomfortable and did not press my request for a vote.

Mathew John, who had left college after finishing his degree, came to meet me. He had also joined the SCF, and our friendship had significantly influenced his decision to join us. "I would have loved to come and campaign for you," he said, "but I am now running pillar to post searching for a job." His family was not well off and depended on him to land a job and support them financially. "You are not likely to win as an SCF candidate, and I am sure I will also lose if contesting under this banner, but I wish you all the best!"

The campaigning got intense, and the various groups inside the campus took out spirited processions. One day, the jathas of the Congress and Janatha came close to each other, leading to skirmishes. Violent fisticuffs ensued, and things seemed poised for an all-out battle.

Robin was with me, trying to muster enough of our members for our own procession, which could never match the other groups in numbers. "We'll go in and separate them," he exclaimed, and we rushed in between the two clashing groups and, holding our hands to form two human chains, pushed the groups apart. Though fewer in numbers, nobody messed up with the SCF guys, and we succeeded in getting them to spread apart. The incident gained us much appreciation even among the teachers, and we were not looked down upon as before.

My brother, who was in the first year of his degree course, campaigned against me. The previous year, he had worked for my victory. His stand was that he could not accept my defection to another party, especially the communist nonbelievers. However, this did not go down well with my mother, who had by then reconciled to the change in my political affiliation.

During dinner one day, she confronted him. "I heard you are campaigning against your elder brother. It doesn't look good for us as a family."

I came to his defense. "Can't people have different political views? Is it possible for all family members to have the same views on everything? Let him continue as he wishes."

And so he continued actively campaigning for my defeat with far greater intensity than I worked for my own success. He could earn a name for himself as a defender of the Faith, which enabled him to reach great heights in a future political career. We, however, did not let this difference affect our relationship with each other, both of us taking a high moral ground.

I lost the elections, but only by fifty-four votes. I considered it a victory of sorts since the previous SCF candidates had not gotten even a tenth of the votes that I had polled. But not so the other SCF members, especially Robin. They had wanted a win. "It is your fault." Robin was unambiguous. "Your appeal for votes was not emphatic enough."

26. Ticketless Travel

In a way, I was glad I lost, as I could now concentrate on my studies and try to get that medical seat. But there were still eight more months for the exams, so I continued my happy-go-lucky life, cutting classes and playing cards in Sugathan's shop and freaking out to see films with Reji, a junior who lived close to my home.

I couldn't ask for money from my father to see movies, so I would skip lunch for a few days till I had enough money for a film. All the local theatres had mediocre films, whereas Reji and I, being true connoisseurs, preferred to see standard Malayalam and English films; it wouldn't hurt if they were X-rated. We had to go to Kottayam, about 30 km away, where many multiplexes screened such movies.

The best way to reach there was by train, but the fare would mean skipping lunch for another three days. Traveling ticketless was the only way out. The journey took just thirty minutes, so it was unlikely that the TTE (Train Ticket Examiner) would check on us within this time. Once we got down at Kottayam, we could get out through a break in the platform's fencing, avoiding the main gate where someone would be there to check tickets.

After we succeeded a couple of times, we became bolder, and it became a weekly affair. I could get to watch one excellent film every week if I continued to have lunch only on alternate days.

When I reached home in the evening, I would be famished and raid the refrigerator to gobble down whatever leftovers I could get. "Where is all this stuff you eat disappearing?" my mother wondered. "You look as if you are starving!"

One day, I spotted the TTE checking tickets in our compartment and alerted Renji. "Let's go into the bathroom," he whispered back. "We'll stay there till the train stops at Kottayam and then get out fast." The plan worked, and we escaped getting caught.

"What will happen if we get caught?" I asked Reji as we were walking to the theatre.

"We will have to pay a heavy fine; if we can't, they will hand us over to the railway police. They will tonsure our heads before letting us go." It was late by the time we returned home, and I straightaway hit the bed after dinner.

We were going to see the next film by Mel Brooks. As we sat discussing the movie we were about to see, the TTE appeared before us and demanded to see our tickets. I fumbled in my pockets and exclaimed, "It seems I have lost it!" I saw Reji getting up and walking off with the crowd.

The TTE caught my hand in a firm grip. "Don't think you can fool me," he said as he tightened his hold on me. At the station, he handed me over to the Railway Police. There were two of them, both heavily built and sporting large mustaches. They dragged me into a cramped room and sat me on a tall stool in a corner. One of them worked on my head, taking out giant scissors from a table. I tried to struggle, but the other pinned me down with a powerful grip.

My hair fell in a circle around me. It was almost like a barbershop, but there was no mirror, and they did not drape me. They then applied thick lather all over my scalp and, with a large, shiny razor, started shaving off what little stump of hair I had left.

I woke up with a start in a cold sweat. Heart racing, I felt my scalp and realized my hair was still there. Relieved that it was a dream, I went to the kitchen and asked my mother for a coffee.

My dream that day intensified my anxiety about the consequences of being caught. What will my parents say if I come home hairless? I shared my thoughts with Reji, and we reduced our frequency of film trips, always taking a valid train ticket, which meant I had to starve for four to five afternoons to earn enough for a film.

The dangers were not just there. Twice, we missed being caught by our parents. The first time we were walking back to the railway station when we saw a person in a white cassock walking straight towards us. It was my father! My immediate reaction was to turn around and run, but a bus slowed down close to the footpath, and I jumped into it. I could see that my father had spotted Reji and stopped to talk to him. As the bus passed them, I realized I would not have enough for the train fare if I paid even the minimum bus fare. "Please let me out! I've got into the wrong bus," I cried out to the conductor.

He was irritated. "We can't stop every time for each passenger. You can get down at the next stop and walk back from there."

The next stop happened to be the railway station; I got a free ride to my destination and waited for Reji to reach me.

"Smart thing you did, jumping onto that bus," he said. "Your father asked me how I was here, and I told him I came to meet some friends."

The second time, we narrowly escaped from Reji's father. We had gone to see a sexy English movie. Being a bit late, we got seats in the front row of the balcony. While making our way down the steps, Reji suddenly turned around and rushed back. "Get back!" he hissed. "My father is there, sitting in the second row."

We waited outside for the advertisements to end and the lights to go off. As the movie began, we confided our predicament to the guard, who couldn't hide his amusement. He escorted us down the steps with his torch, shielding us from sight with his body. After the film, we stayed in our seats and left only after everyone else had gone.

27. Study Tour

Final exams being just another two months away, most students, especially the girls, started zealous study. We would have a study tour, after which there would be a study leave of one month before the final. I reckoned there would be enough time to finish the syllabus after the study tour.

We were all excited about the tour. It was to be a ten-day trip on our college bus, and we had an exuberant start. The staff members were the acting HOD, Alexander Sir, George Sir, and Jessy Kochamma. We were singing at the top of our voices. The parodies of Christian hymns we rendered disturbed George Sir, but we heeded little. After all, we were on tour.

The study started when we were let out into a forest to collect specimens. Jessy Kochamma showed us how to peel off the outer bark of the massive old trees to reveal a host of creatures living there. We gingerly collected the exotic ones, put them in glass bottles, and took them to Jessy Kochamma, who would identify them with an unpronounceable name. She would specify the ones to preserve and take back to college. We let off those specimens we already had in our department lab to continue their life within the bark of trees.

We went to Ooty. I had a jolly time joking with friends and smoking cigarettes to keep out the cold. The pear did not taste as it did earlier, but the flowers were stunning.

Rameshwaram beach presented us with marine creatures we had only seen in textbooks. We had a veteran local guide, Murugan, a native and postgraduate in Zoology, who led us into the shallow sea. Even after we had gone a kilometer, the water was only knee-deep. The waves were just ripples; ideal conditions for a host of sea animals - starfishes, sea anemones in all the rainbow colors, and hermit crabs crawling slowly, overburdened with heavy shells.

We walked ahead, following our guide. "Want to see a Portuguese Man Of War?" he asked, pointing to the blue bottle jellyfish with its gas-filled float resembling an old warship with sails full. *How does he know where to find each specimen?*

Our next stop, Mahe, was a place where liquor was so cheap that it cost just a third of the price in our state. We bought as much as we could afford. Though illegal to take out of the state, we reckoned they would not check a college bus with students on a study tour.

As we reached the interstate check-post, an officer stopped our bus, and we could hear him ask the driver to open the door for him to check inside. Frantic, we looked for any place to hide the bottles. "Give it here," one girl said and stuffed it down her sweater. The other girls grabbed the remaining bottles and pushed them into their vests. The officers were stern and thorough when they went through the bus and our luggage, but didn't body-check the girls.

There was a week before the month-long study leave for the final exams. We had a farewell gathering before the classes ended. The girls sang a parody with me as the prime target of ridicule. The teachers gave brief speeches with lots of advice and asked us to be in contact even after leaving college.

I rose to speak, representing all the students. I started well, but when searching for words to express myself, I had a flood of memories of our good times together. The possibility that we might not meet again crossed my mind, and I broke down, unable to complete my speech.

"I think I now understand you more than ever," George Sir said, patting me. "You said sorry if you have caused trouble for us teachers, and I think I should also say sorry for misunderstanding you on many occasions."

They called me to the office a few days before college closed for study leave. I was surprised to see my father sitting in the Principal's office, looking grim. "You don't have the requisite attendance to appear for the public exam," the Principal announced. "While you need eighty percent attendance, you have barely thirty-five!" I stood silent, head bowed.

The head of our department walked in. "He is a good student, though he tends to cut classes. He has come first in all our internal tests. It will be a pity if he can't write the University exams," he said.

The Principal pondered for a moment and looked at my father. "There is only one way out. Produce a medical certificate showing some illness which required rest for about forty-five days."

"Nothing doing!" My father was adamant. "If he is not eligible to write the exams this year, let him do it next year."

Back home, he asked me. "You were going every day from here. Where were you going if not to college?"

"I was indeed going to college," I said, "but some classes were so boring that I bunked them and sat in the library. I cannot understand how I am so short in attendance."

A few days later, we received a message from the college office informing us that there had been a mistake, and I indeed had the bare minimum attendance to write the exam. I learned later that my Professor had convinced the Principal to make alterations in the attendance register to give me the minimum required.

28. Final Exam

The study leave period started, and I began in earnest. I arranged all the books subject-wise and started with Taxonomy, the classification of all members of the animal kingdom- right from the lowly single-celled animals like amoeba to the mighty elephant. They classified the multicellular animals into those with a backbone and those without. Ironically Homo Sapiens (humans) are classified under Vertebrates, meaning those with a spine.

As I went through the tongue-twisting terminology, I felt my head throbbing. Soon I started having chills, and I realized I had a high fever. I closed my books to get a pill of Paracetamol and lay down. The sweating that followed drenched my clothes, and I was fatigued. I felt nauseated and could not eat lunch, and by evening started vomiting. It was the beginning of several bouts to follow, and by night, I was famished.

My father took me to Dr. George's Hospital early the next morning. There was a large crowd waiting. Seeing my condition, they called me in before my turn. Dr. George felt my temperature with the back of his hand, checked my pulse, and pressed over my abdomen while still sitting and asked. "Have you traveled outside the state recently?"

"Yes," my father replied. "He returned from a ten-day college study tour only last week."

"It is typhoid," Dr. George declared without a doubt. "I think it will be better to admit him."

Even today, I wonder how he could make this diagnosis without a lab test or a thorough examination.

"I would like to keep him at home," my father replied. "Please prescribe the required medicines, and I will nurse him myself."

"Okay then," Dr. George said as he prescribed two injections and a large bundle of tablets.

There were a lot of chloramphenicol capsules I had to take every two hours. My stomach burned, for which I took antacids. Still, I used to throw up frequently. The fever was unrelenting. By the fifth day, I felt relief and could think and talk clearly. *Will I be able to write the exam this year? When will I be able to study? Is there any chance of me making it to the medical entrance?*

My stomach was still on fire- I wondered whether it was from the disease or the capsules I was taking. "Do I have to continue these medicines? My stomach is aching," I told my father when he brought me the next dose of tablets.

"Of course!" he replied. "You should be grateful that we are having these medicines now. In my childhood, getting typhoid either meant death or permanent disability, like loss of sight or hearing."

He told me my Professor had contacted him over the phone and asked whether I had typhoid. Nineteen others from my class had the same disease, all in some hospital or other. It took them some days and a battery of tests to confirm the diagnosis and start specific treatment for all the others. "Seems all of you were buying and eating snacks and ice cream from the roadside?"

It was true. The department was in a PR exercise as it received complaints from parents about the staff members who were not careful in keeping their wards safe from disease. However, the authorities pointed out that the staff members also took food from the same hotels, but none were affected.

I received several get-well letters and cheer-up notes from my classmates. Our teachers regularly enquired about my health with my father over the phone, and Jessy Kochamma sent a message with some books for me to read. Spiritual people projected as men of science wrote most of them, all trying to disprove the theory of evolution.

Jessy Kochamma had shown her displeasure while teaching this theory during class. That was all she could do, as professional ethics bound her to teach what they gave in the syllabus. I read through them all but didn't find the reasonings very convincing, and I found Darwin was more believable and told my father so.

"Since you are reading so much, maybe you can start studying bit by bit," my father suggested.

I dug out my textbooks and started earnestly but couldn't continue. I developed a throbbing in my head. "This is not like reading other books. I have a headache and can't concentrate," I told my father.

"Okay, let's wait another week for you to recover," my father agreed. When I resumed my studies, exams were just six days ahead, and I had no hope of completing the portions. I selected some parts usually asked in the exams, leaving out the rest.

Those unaffected by the disease had already completed the first revision round and started on the second. I invited Thomas George to stay with me to have a combined study, and he was happy. My father allowed us to use the guest room of the Bible Institute kept for visiting bishops and other dignitaries. They didn't expect to need it for another two weeks, so we settled down with the books. We persisted until the early morning hours, sleeping more during the day.

By the time the exams started, I had recovered from typhoid, and my appetite was voracious. About a third of the questions were from portions I had left out, but I did not leave them blank. I wrote detailed answers based on what little I knew, adding up with a lot of my imagination.

Practicals were two weeks later. I was tasked with opening up a frog and dissecting and exposing its nervous system. I got it right and displayed it nicely. As the external examiner approached my table, I heard Jessy Kochamma put in a word of recommendation. "He is our best student, and we expected him to qualify for a medical seat. But he got typhoid after our study tour and was in bed during the study leave."

The examiner looked at me somewhat skeptically and seemed irritated by the recommendation. He started firing questions at me. I was familiar with the frog's nervous system and answered readily. He then switched to other topics, and I saw his face change to appreciation. "Good," he commented and moved on to the next table.

After the dissected specimens were evaluated, it was time for the spotters. I knew all the specimens kept in our lab, having been seeing them for the past three years, and I was prompt in my answers. "Very good!" the examiner seemed pleased.

Hopes of getting a medical seat resurfaced after the practicals. Going by the examiner's response, I should get good marks.

With the exams over, I now lounged at home waiting for the results to know my fate. I missed college and my friends there. The only solace was the evening sojourns at the YMCA. We spent our time with heated arguments on serious issues, most often about the unforgivable mistakes committed during our game of '56,' the engaging card game.

"You will make it to Medical College and make us all proud," the fellows there cheered me up. "You are going to be the only doctor among us. Once your admission is confirmed, you have to give us a splendid treat."

"Sure," I agreed.

Around that time, a wild idea for a long cycle trip emerged and gripped our minds.

29. Kerala to Tamilnadu

We were animated as we planned the details. We appointed Avaran and Georgie as the maintenance crew for the trip. They went to 'Manian's' cycle repair shop to learn the basics of bicycle maintenance and came back armed with puncture repairing kits and tools for tightening the cycle chain and nuts.

The plan was to travel to Kanyakumari and back in six days. Kanyakumari (in translation, 'The Virgin Princess') was the southernmost tip of India and was 215 kilometers from our location, Thiruvalla. We charted out the route and decided where we would spend the nights. They appointed me as the medical officer. 'Since you are the only person amongst us who plans to be a doctor.'

Fortunately, MK, now in his third year as a medical student, was at home, and I went to him for advice. He suggested I stock some Paracetamol tablets for fever, antacids for gastritis, Perinorm tablets for vomiting, and Lomotil for diarrhea. He also recommended sterile dressing materials and antiseptic ointments for injuries.

The nagging fear that my parents wouldn't allow me to go on the trip was at the back of my mind. My fears were not misplaced. When I asked my father's permission for the tour, he agreed immediately but backtracked as soon as he learned that we were planning to go on bicycles.

"Why bicycles? Take a bus; there are so many going that way. Cycling all this way will be dangerous."

"But that won't be any fun!" I pleaded. "We had planned on a bicycle trip. I want to go!"

We kept the issue festering while I went about arranging for the trip. I packed my bag and gave the cycle to Manian's shop for servicing. Before leaving, I asked my father for a hundred rupees for my expenses.

"But I told you not to go!"

"But I want to go. I will forever regret it if I don't make this trip!"

My father took his time before he agreed. "You should be very careful. Stick to the side of the road and go at a slow and steady pace."

My mother was horrified. "You mean to say that you are allowing him to make this long trip on cycle? What if he falls sick? We won't even know if something happens to him!"

"He is not going alone," my father replied. "I am sure his friends will help each other if any problems arise." Appachen had made up his mind, and I was elated.

We planned to start on a Friday afternoon and travel to Kottarakkara, 50 km away. Our friend Abu, who worked there, shared a room with a colleague who volunteered to go home that day to accommodate us.

We packed our bags on the back carriers of our cycles. Mine was the oldest cycle- an English Raleigh that my father has used for over twenty years. It was a rugged and robust bone-shaker.

We decided on sleeveless banians as our uniform. Six of these, with six underwears, a single pair of trousers, and a lungi to wear at night made up our wardrobe. We also took some steel plates, glasses, and light bedding, as we could not expect to find proper lodging everywhere.

Avaran and Georgie carried the bicycle maintenance tools and the air pump. We put a signboard on the front handle of each cycle with the words 'Kerala-Tamilnadu' on them.

A small crowd gathered at the YMCA to see us off. We looked like a bunch of adventurers as we set out. Tiredness and aching of the legs started after the first twenty kilometers, and we stopped at a roadside pan shop to have lemon juice. "Do you think we will make the entire distance?" Manoj wondered aloud. I was already having doubts.

"Certainly!" Avaran was confidence personified. "Once we get used to it, cycling won't seem so difficult. Come on. We don't have all day! Only thirty kilometers more, and we should get to Kottarakkara for dinner."

After what seemed like never-ending pedaling, we came upon a signboard showing- 'Kottarakkara - 5 km.' We all perked up and picked up speed and soon reached the spot where we were to meet our friend. Keeping the bicycles parked by the side of the road, we waited. A young man saw us and came running over, excited. "Great! Are you guys going to bike all the way to Tamilnadu? Where in Tamilnadu? From where are you coming?"

His enthusiasm was infectious. He wanted us to go with him and be his guests for dinner. We declined politely, saying that we had already made arrangements. Abu turned up just then, apologizing for being late. Our new friend seemed crestfallen. We let him buy ice creams for us, and he left a happy man, wishing us the best of luck.

Abu had set up an expansive dinner for us, but we were all too tired to be hungry, and the ice cream had spoilt whatever appetite we had. We spread our beddings and lay cramped together on the floor. We slept early to set off at daybreak the next day when there would be no traffic to hamper our progress and no sun to tire us down.

As Avaran, who had his alarm watch set, got up and poked us awake, Aliyan sat up groaning and clutched his knees. "I can't continue a bit. My knees are aching. You guys go ahead, and I'll get back to Tiruvalla once I have rested enough."

No amount of coaxing and cajoling could change his decision. We bid him goodbye and set off by 5 a.m. We had cycled for about an hour, and dawn was breaking when we heard a persistent cycle bell ringing. Looking back, we could see a bicycle approaching at breakneck speed. It was Aliyan!

"I felt so bad when you guys left, so after a few moments, I changed my mind and quickly got ready and raced after you.

"But what about your knees?" Avaran inquired.

"They are okay now. After a few hundred meters of pedaling, the pain vanished. It might have been just a bit of stiffness."

We continued our journey, witnessing the unfolding of the new day. Regular folks also started appearing on the roads. Men carrying various tools and implements on their shoulders walked briskly in groups- probably farmworkers on the way to their work sites. Guys with large milk pails on either side of their scooters sped by. Big lorries laden with all sorts of cargo - vegetables, cattle, and huge overflowing bundles of hay raced past, their drivers and helpers waving to us encouragingly.

We spotted an elderly man selling coffee from a large container on an old bicycle. We were already hungry and stopped to have a cup. It tasted lovely, and I felt terrific and asked for another cup. The others also had two cups each, and as we paid him, he accepted the cash with both hands and caressed it to his bowed forehead before keeping it in the cash box.

"Please be careful on your way," he implored. "Always keep a safe distance from the buses and lorries. There will be plenty of them on the road from now on."

The traffic increased to a frenzied chaos- the speeding buses and lorries passing us seemed too close for comfort. Just two days back, as a last-minute attempt to dissuade me from the trip, my mother described how she had seen me being run over by a lorry in a dream. I kept as close to the road's edge as possible, and people walking there gave me a mean look.

Our progress slowed to a crawl after breakfast of idlis (fluffy steamed cakes of rice and lentil) and sambar (a curry of dal and vegetables) from a roadside shack. The sun beat us down, and we were sweating like crazy, leaving a trail of sweat on the road behind us. No amount of water seemed enough.

We pulled up at a roadside paan shop to drink some fresh lime juice, and the young shopkeeper advised us that adding a little salt with the sugar was more rejuvenating. He proved right. We stopped at a paan shop every half hour, most of which had nothing but paan, cigarettes, beedies, and lemon juice.

As we parked at the next paan shop, we saw that this one was different. It was of the same standard wooden enclosure but an array of displayed goodies- magazines, bottles of Coca-Cola, and large glass containers with various delicacies. While ordering our usual lemon juices, I noticed a bottle of white liquid stashed in front and inquired about it.

"That is buttermilk," the guy in a trendy T-shirt handling the shop replied. "Why don't you try it? It is cheaper than lemon juice. We make it from diluted yogurt, adding salt, green chilies, ginger, shallots, and curry leaves. I think it will be much more refreshing for you."

The rejuvenation was unmistakable, and we all had two glasses after the lemonade. Buttermilk became our staple refreshment drink throughout the trip.

The friendly shop handler sold Avaran a comb he had forgotten to bring. Some snacks for the evening drinks, and we spent many times more than our usual stop. "That's the way to run a business. We should learn from him." Avaran was all praise for the shop and its owner as we continued our way.

30. The Virgin Princess

We had a late lunch in another small nondescript hotel by the roadside. It was a small thatched house with a kitchen and a wide veranda with benches and desks for the customers. "Do you want any special dish to go with the meals?" the shopkeeper asked. "We have fried mackerel."

We had them with the meals served to us in banana leaves. Burping our contentment, we asked him if we could sit here and rest for some time before we departed.

"Sure!" he said. "Better that you have a quick nap. Lunchtime is over, and the next customers will come only by tea time." The three benches and three desks he had were just enough for the six of us. The shopkeeper spread out old newspapers over the desks and benches, and we lay down on them and soon fell asleep. We woke up to the sound of customers coming in for tea.

"Can we also have tea before we leave?" I asked. Everyone agreed, and we had tea with hot and crispy vadas. We were contented as we left the place. The bill for lunch, tea, and snacks came to less than two rupees a person.

"What a waste, going to fancy hotels. Can we ever dream of having food so tasty?" remarked Boban as we got back on our cycles.

"He will never be a successful business person like that guy in the paan shop," Avaran observed. "He won't earn much in his entire life, but what a delightful fellow!"

"At the end of the day, he might be the happier man," Boban observed philosophically.

Our destination was the Neyyar Dam, where we were to spend the night. We no longer saw shops or houses as we raced across the lonely road to the dam. It was a shrubby forest with few trees. We had been warned that wild elephants might cross our path, so we rushed to reach our destination before it got too dark.

When we came upon the sign 'Neyyar Dam - 10 km,' it was like an energy booster. The grueling day's end was in sight. We picked up the pace and pedaled like one possessed, accelerating to the maximum possible speed.

It was already dark when we reached the government-run dormitory where we were to stay for the night. We quickly finished a bottle of rum, washed and changed, had dinner at the canteen, and got into bed. "No need to get up early morning tomorrow. Let us relax, see around, and set off after breakfast," Avaran announced before pulling the blanket over his head.

We cycled to the dam in the morning. The air was white with mist, and our breaths were like smoke. Standing on the dam, we could see below the vast expanse of the catchment lake and the banks on either side. After a few feet of bare land, it was a thick forest.

Taking in this breathtaking scene, I noticed that the boulders on the bank to our right seemed to move. "Look! Elephants!" someone shouted. The wild elephants, no bigger than footballs from that distance, frolicked with abandon on the bank, some getting into the water and spraying it on themselves with their trunks.

We rushed off after breakfast as we could not afford to miss the sunset at Kanyakumari. We traveled several kilometers downhill without having to pedal even once. Once we reached the plains, we plodded on with renewed vigor. Pedaling didn't seem much of a strain anymore. Fortified with buttermilk many times along the way, we made good progress.

As we entered the state of Tamil Nadu, the difference in the landscape was striking. The thick canopy of trees gave way to vast stretches of barren land dotted here and there with palm trees and interspersed with patches of vegetable cultivation.

Food tasted very different and bland, with white rice of small grains in place of the big rice with brown streaks we were used to having. The sun was hotter here, and even the buttermilk was waning in its efficacy. We were exhausted when we reached Kanyakumari and checked into the Vivekananda Center, where we were to stay.

We had to rush out so as not to miss the sunset. The backside of the lodge overlooked the sea, and we just had to reach there. We made it just minutes before the sun's final descent into the sea. It was a magnificent sight, with the sky painted in vivid colors of all hues and the sea reflecting them, adding its greenish-blue tinge. We could view the luminous orange globe descending into the sea at the horizon, the background lighting building up a crescendo to the climax before the lights slowly dimmed for the darkness to take over.

The visual treat was a powerful tonic that soothed our bodies' weary bones. We lay down to sleep after a heavy supper. We had to get up early the next day to catch the sunrise. (Kanyakumari is one of the few places on earth where you can watch sunrise and sunset from the same spot.)

After the spectacular sunset last night, the sunrise was disappointing because thick clouds played spoilsport, covering the sun as it emerged from the sea. We could only catch glimpses of it through breaks in the clouds, colored in a red hue.

We watched until the sun emerged from the clouds and took on its fiery yellow face. As it warmed up, we left to prepare for our return journey.

31. Heroes, Ourselves

It was a small hotel near the market that we got into for breakfast. People came up to ask us about our adventures, and Avaran gave them a briefing in what Tamil he could muster. As we finished our food and asked for the bill, the owner declared he was not charging us, as he wanted it to be a treat. While thanking him, we noticed a commotion outside.

A crowd had gathered to see us, and people jostled to get near and ask questions as we came out. They stared at us as if we had come from another planet. The mob became so thick that we couldn't get to our bicycles parked outside. People were inspecting our cycles as if they were some newly invented machines.

Hearing the commotion, two policemen appeared and made way for us through the throng. It boosted our egos, being escorted by police officers through a crowd of fans. As we got on our bikes and started moving, a loud cheer broke out from the group, and we responded by waving to them until they were out of sight.

We spent the night in Kovalam, the famous beach in Trivandrum. We took shelter in a shack near the beach. The family who owned it lived in a hut a little further away. They brought us supper wrapped up in banana leaves. It had the unique taste of homemade food and had rice, prawns, avial (mixed vegetable dish), and coconut chutney.

It was cramped inside the hut, so we lay outside for some time before bed. We spread the mats on the dry beach sand and lay watching the stars above and the occasional meteor streaking across the sky. I don't know when we drifted off to sleep, but we were awakened by water lapping on our feet several hours later. It was the changing tide that had brought the water up till there. Before we could figure it out, a gigantic wave came crashing, drenching us with salty water.

We gathered our mats and ran inside. Toweling ourselves dry, we stretched on the bare floor as all our mats and bed sheets were drenched and fell into a deep sleep. I felt the chill from the bare floor. Waking up the next day, we saw the sea had taken up the place where we had been lying.

We spent the day in Kovalam, frolicking and walking along the beach. The sight of bare-chested foreign women caused considerable excitement.

"If these foreigners can expose thus, why can't our local girls do the same?" Boban wondered. "I wish I could see at least one Malayali woman like this!"

"What if it's your sister or your future wife?" Aliyan asked, and Boban was silent.

The native women were covered in sarees, even while swimming or wading in the water. *When God condemned Adam and Eve to be ashamed of their nakedness, the curse fell heavily on our people.*

We set off from Kovalam by early evening, planning to cycle throughout the night as it would be less tiring. Problems started when Kunjumon had a cough and felt tired. I felt his skin and found it very warm. I gave him a tablet of Paracetamol and some cough syrup. It seemed to work wonders, and he reported feeling all right soon.

We reached the capital city, Trivandrum, by late evening. There was a lot of traffic, but most vehicles gave us respectful space, seeing our convoy. As we reached the main traffic junction, the policeman stopped all other cars and signaled us to cross; another boost to our inflated egos, since we've seen this being done only for VIPs.

We got into a vegetarian restaurant opposite the grand white Secretariat building, the state government's headquarters, which housed the Legislative Assembly. "We won't be stopping for dinner, so have your full, enough to last till tomorrow morning," Avaran advised.

I stuffed myself with a two-foot-long masala dosa and a plate of poories. *How tasty are these vegetarian dishes if prepared well!* After the food, we had coffee and asked for the bill. A crowd had gathered outside, and some were inspecting our bikes. The server who had gone to collect our bill was in a long conversation with the manager. We wondered what the confusion was about.

The manager rose from his chair and came to us. "We are not billing you," he said. "Please consider it a compliment from us, and best wishes for the successful completion of your tour." We left, thanking him. It was a significant amount that we saved by his generosity.

Avaran complained of nausea and discomfort in his stomach, which aggravated so much that we had to stop. I gave him some antacids and a Perinorm tablet, and we resumed our journey. But after a short distance, Avaran halted his bike, rushed to the edge of the road, sat down, and started vomiting.

I patted him on the back, hoping it would relieve him somewhat. He again threw up a watery and bilious mass with another violent surge. After another bout, he leaned back on me. "We have to get to a proper doctor," he croaked, trying to make it sound funny with an apology of a laugh.

We were in luck. As we asked a passerby, he pointed to a side road nearby. "You just have to go about a hundred meters to reach Maya Clinic. Dr. Adarsh will be there. He is excellent."

The clinic was a three-room affair. The doctor was in the consulting room, getting ready to close up and leave. "You don't seem to have any infection; you are not running a fever," he said as he read the thermometer he had kept in Avaran's armpit. "I suppose it is just gastritis. Did you have much to drink last night?"

"Yes, I think I had a bit too much," Avaran replied sheepishly.

"I will give you an injection and start an IV drip. You should be okay. I am leaving for home now, which is just nearby. They will call me if needed."

There were two nurses, a pretty young girl and a middle-aged lady- both beautiful souls. We all stood around the bed, watching each drop fall, eager to get going. It took an hour for the fluid to run out.

I wandered around, taking in the setup. Avaran lay in the large room with three beds. An enclosed space marked 'Minor Surgery,' with a high desk inside, was at its side. At the entrance was a spacious corridor with waiting chairs. On one corner was a shelf stacked with patients' files, and behind it was another sizeable wooden shelf stocked with medicines. *I should have a clinic like this if I get to be a doctor.*

After the drip, we were glad to get the bill from Sr. Pretty (Yes, that was her real name too!), mainly because the total bill was just twelve rupees.

Back on our cycles, Avaran was energetic. "I feel as fit as ever," he declared. "Thanks to that doctor."

It was dark, and we were on a narrow stretch of road we had taken as a shortcut to the National Highway. It was a mud road littered with stones and pebbles, and the ride was slow and bumpy. We heard a hissing sound from Regi's cycle, which he stopped immediately. It was a bad puncture.

"Damn! This will take at least half an hour to set right," Avaran cursed as he laid out the tools and started working on it with Georgie. It was a desolate place with a closed paan shop by the road and a black Ambassador car parked nearby. A lonely street bulb gave us some visibility.

The rest of us walked around, trying to find someplace where we could rest. I climbed onto a desk before the paan shop, stretched myself, and fell asleep. Almost three-quarters of an hour had passed when they woke me up to resume our journey, but Boban was nowhere to be seen. His cycle stood near where the car, which I had heard starting and going off while half asleep, had been.

"Now, where the hell is he?" Avaran became anxious, and we started shouting out for him into the empty night. Getting no response, we became desperate and shouted for him in unison, our voices getting frantic. The lights went on in the nearby houses, and two people came toward us.

"Why are you people creating such a ruckus in the night?" They seemed very irritated but softened upon hearing our story and joined in the search. "There is no place here where he can hide, even if he wanted to. It is a mystery!"

An approaching car interrupted us. It was the same car that was parked there earlier. Boban emerged from the back with a sheepish grin.

"Now, if you ever feel sleepy again, find someplace other than my car!" shouted the man behind the wheel as he turned the car around and sped away.

Boban related to us the happenings. Looking for a place to lie down, he found the car door not locked, so he got in and lay down on the back seat. He was fast asleep when the man got in and drove away. After some time, when the car took a sharp turn, he slid off and fell to the floor, waking up with a shout. The driver got the fright of his life, and he just managed to avoid the car crashing into a tree.

He gave Boban his mind in the choicest of words while driving him back to us. "You should have seen his face when he caught sight of me," Boban chuckled. "As if he'd seen a ghost!"

Our tensions gave way to mirth as we continued on our trek. "A real nice gentleman. We should be thankful that he didn't chuck out Boban and just carried on. So kind of him to bring him back to us," Aliyan opined.

Soon, we rejoined the broad highway and cruised along. It was hours past midnight, and sleep became overpowering. Jolted awake by a pothole on the road, I realized I had been pedaling half asleep for the past few minutes. "Hey guys, I think I slept off for some time!" I shouted to the others.

"Me too!" said Georgie.

"Wow, that's dangerous!" Avaran responded. "I think we should rest for some time. This road seems wide enough. We will lay our mats on the side and try to catch a nap."

It was a straight stretch of road, with vast expanses of land on either side. Lorries raced past in both directions. "We have to make sure we don't get run over by one of them," Avaran said. We created a wall of cycles around the area where we had spread our mats and draped them with light-colored sheets.

"They must be blind to run over us now."

"But they also could be drunk or sleep off while driving, as we did just now." I still had my doubts.

"In that case, lying down here will be much safer than cycling on the road; that risk is always there. Come on, try to catch a few hours' sleep," Avaran said as he stretched out on the mat and cuddled up with a pillow. We all followed.

I dreamt of lorries going over me- several ones of different makes and colors. My mother watched in horror as they approached me, but they all passed over me, causing no harm. The miraculous escape amazed me each time till I realized I had shrunk in size to a small boy- as small as the schoolchild who fell on the road in Bombay.

32. Triumphant Return

"Hello! Are you guys okay?" Someone was calling out. We woke up one by one, rubbing our eyes. The orange-yellow light of the sun shone on a group of early morning joggers, now gaping at us across the wall of cycles. There were ladies too, and I hastily wrapped my lungi into place to be decent enough.

We explained our story while getting back on our bikes without changing and sped away. Someone called out for three cheers to the bikers, and shouts of 'hip, hip, hurray!' resounded behind us.

We felt famished and pulled up at the nearest hotel that we saw open. "Breakfast will take at least half an hour to be ready," the man at the counter informed us.

I felt my morning urges. "Is there a toilet I could use?" I asked, clutching my belly. "Me too!" most everyone echoed.

"There is only one common toilet down here," the manager

informed. "But we have a few rooms upstairs for rent." We asked if we could take two rooms for an hour. "The minimum period for renting out the space is for a day," he said.

The urge to relieve ourselves was so intense that we took two rooms. We refreshed and changed and went down to have a breakfast of steaming appams (rice pancakes) with egg roast. We finished the food, savoring each bite, and approached the counter to pay the bill. "That will be six rupees," he said with a smile. "I am not charging you for the rooms."

We were now on our last lap. We hoped to reach back in Tiruvalla by evening. Cycling was not a tiring activity for us now; it was as natural as walking. We kept up a fast and steady pace.

We arrived back at the YMCA in Tiruvalla early in the evening. All friends and YMCA officials had gathered there to plan a reception for us. When we rode in, they were busy discussing how to receive us with some refreshments and mementos. We had turned up much earlier than expected, so they dropped further plans.

The President of the YMCA came out to see our bikes and was upset about the signboards with Kerala-Tamilnadu written on them. "You should have written YMCA, Tiruvalla, and we could have sponsored your trip!"

"You knew about our trip but said nothing about this before we set out," we replied. He did not broach the subject further.

We spent some time relating stories of our trip to the friends who had gathered. A few of them who had planned to join, but backed out later, could not hide their disappointment. I requested permission to use the telephone in the YMCA and called home to inform them we had returned. My father seemed very relieved to hear from me.

We felt sad that the trip had ended, and we itched to get back on the cycle. Boban came up with an idea. "There is a new Hindi film at Aswathi Theatres in Changanachery. What about going there on our cycles? It is just a ride of six kilometers." All six of us were quick to agree. Six kilometers was kid stuff for us who had just cycled above four hundred!

"You guys rode all this way, and still, you are not tired?" Roji asked, amazed. "I want to join, but not on a cycle! I'll bring my bike." Many more wanted to join but were skeptical about using the bicycles. There were two motorcycles available.

We set off as a convoy of eight bicycles (two more had become bold enough to try) and two motorbikes. The bikes carried three people each, and two of us took pillion riders on the bicycles, so fourteen guys traveled to Changanachery. The two freshers struggled to keep pace with us.

We knew even before the start that the film would be a flop, as we made up more than half of the entire audience.

We met at the YMCA the next day, in the evening, to settle the expenses for the trip. Thanks to all the free food we received on the way and the savings on room rent for two days (Abu's hospitality on the first day and by sleeping on the road on the last), our total expenses for the six-day trip were only eighty-two rupees per person. I felt it was the most worthy money ever spent in my life, as each of us received a balance of eighteen rupees.

33. Fate in the Balance

I grew apprehensive with each passing day as the date for publication of the exam results drew near. If it were not for that damned typhoid fever just before the exams, I would have gotten enough marks, I thought ruefully. Anyway, I could blame typhoid for not getting admission this time too.

The cut-off for medical entrance was 82 percent in the previous year, which usually increased by two to three percent each year. I reckoned I would make it if I scored above 85 percent, which was unlikely: my self-evaluation had presented me with just about 82 percent.

A week later, the mark list came in, and I scored 84 percent. I resigned myself to another narrow miss, though a flicker of hope persisted. It would take several weeks for the final list of successful medical applicants. I wondered if I should join the dental course if it were all I would be eligible for this time too. But I could have done that three years ago!

Reservation for postgraduates would be only for one more year, after which all medical entrances would be through a competitive exam. I would not benefit from a postgraduate degree by finishing my MSc in another two years, and the only option would be to write the competitive exams with fresh pre-degree pass-outs who would be five years younger than me.

I could not take chances, so I applied and got selected for MSc in Zoology at the University College at Trivandrum. I was first on the selection list when I reported for the joining interview.

"This is a waste of our time," one professor in the interview panel remarked as they completed the formalities to enroll me. "These people will soon come for a transfer certificate from here to join Medical College." *I wish I could be as confident as him.*

After a few weeks, news got around that the list of successful candidates was to be published in the Medical College office in Trivandrum on the coming Monday. I traveled to Trivandrum to reach there by Sunday evening and traced out MK and caught up on him just coming out of the hospital.

He was wearing a white coat with a stethoscope hanging around his neck and was surprised to see me. "I thought about you, knowing they will put the final list out tomorrow, but I never thought you would be bold enough to come here alone. Don't let it out that you are an aspiring candidate. If someone finds out, your ordeal in ragging will start right now! And by the way, you will get in. I heard that the minimum percentage of marks required has come down this year."

MK persuaded me to stay with him in the hostel that night. "We will have dinner at the Coffee House, as I don't want to risk taking you to our mess. Others may find out you are a future student. After dinner, we will walk to the college office, and I will show you where they put up the list. You can come and check tomorrow. I will have to attend clinics by eight o'clock in the morning."

The Coffee House was teeming with men and women in white coats- all medical students and doctors. Many were acquaintances of MK and came up to us. He introduced me as a friend from his hometown. "It's good that you look older and mature, and nobody suspected you of being an aspiring medical student," he remarked.

As we came out of the Coffee House, I could see screaming ambulances speeding in to park in front of the casualty of the Medical College Hospital, which was just opposite. "It seems there has been some mass casualty, and many are injured," MK said as he led me through the main gate into the sprawling campus. There were enormous buildings on either side of the road, and MK identified them to me

As we walked further, the buildings gave way to open spaces. There was a large football ground with a cricket pitch in the middle. Beyond this ground, I could make out another small ground with basketball posts. On the farther side of the football field, tall steps separated it from the higher ground with the college building, making it a gallery.

Tall trees at the edges had overhanging branches, giving shade to those sitting on the steps. I could see a few couples with their arms thrown over each other. As we walked further, the extensive building of the college came into view. There was a vast lawn with neatly trimmed buffalo grass in front. "Do you want to go in and see the classrooms?" MK enquired.

"Naw," I said. "I will see it later if I get admission."

"You are a doubting Thomas!" MK remarked. "I tell you, it will be a cakewalk with your marks."

MK led me down a slope to the left, which led to the office building. The ground floor was the library, and I saw it was still open. Students were inside, immersed in their textbooks. We climbed the stairs to see the room with 'Principal' written above the door.

"That's where they will put up the list tomorrow," MK said, pointing to a prominent notice board with glass doors locked with a small padlock. The inside was lined with a green felt cloth pinned with pieces of paper with various notifications. "This place is likely to have a heavy crowd tomorrow."

I noticed a colorful poster on the wall next to the notice board. It had the WHO emblem, with a picture of a young girl and a proclamation that Small Pox has been eradicated worldwide. I looked at the picture for a long time, and the image became blurred as the uncanny resemblance to Leelamol sank in, and my eyes became moist.

I realized the next day that what MK told me was an understatement. The entire area was teeming with people, and as I pushed myself through to the staircase, I saw it was jam-packed. *How will the Principal get to his office today?* They had not put up the list yet.

I went outside and waited for the commotion to subside. I noticed the sidewall of a culvert by the roadside, shaded by a thick canopy of bamboo trees, and sat there, watching the people. Soon, there was a clamor and a rush into the office. They had published the list!

People were coming out after checking the results. I could know who got admission and who did not just by watching their faces. The majority had gloomy faces, while others were exuberant. One young fellow was jumping, pumping the air with his fists.

More than an hour later, the crowd diminished somewhat, and I went in to check my fate. I could feel my heart pumping as I scanned the list from the bottom upwards, expecting a narrow win. My heart sank as my eyes moved up along the list. I had almost reached the middle of the list, and my name was nowhere to be seen.

I started again, this time going slow and thorough; even so, I could not spot my name. Frustrated, I scanned almost to the top of the list, and my name was there in the 43rd slot! I rubbed my eyes and looked again; It was still there!

I ran down the steps, elbowing through the crowd. I felt like shaking my fist in the air and jumping like the boy I had seen earlier, but I restrained myself. I hurried back through the campus to reach the central junction and called my father from a telephone booth. He was overjoyed. "Go visit your grandmother and inform her," he said. "You can stay there today and come back home tomorrow."

Grandma was out in the courtyard cutting wood logs into smaller chunks for firewood with an axe as big as her. I watched, fascinated, as her deft blows cut through the wood, sleeving off splinters just the right size for the fireplace. I broke the news to her.

"Good," she responded with little excitement. "I knew all along that you would make it." Though glad, she showed no surprise. Keeping the axe aside, she went inside the house to bring me two pieces of dried banana fruit. She then lit the fire and put the kettle on it. "Have a bath and change. Tea will be ready by then."

After tea, I went to the paddy field and walked across to my uncle's house to tell them the news. I noticed the stream was just a trickle.

The next day, as I was taking leave of grandma, she handed me a ten-rupee note as a present. "Don't spend them on cigarettes," she warned me. She had a piece of parting advice as she bid me farewell. "Study well and become a good doctor. And always be careful with scissors. Don't leave them in anyone's abdomen."

34. The Celebration

My friends at the YMCA did not doubt that my selection warranted an elaborate treat. "It is the first time anyone from our group got selected for a medical seat," Avaran pointed out.

I committed nothing then but later asked my father if he could give me some money to give a party to my friends. "How many are there?" he asked.

"Around twenty," I said, exaggerating the numbers a bit to make sure the funds allotted will be adequate.

"Twenty! Okay, I will give you hundred rupees. Keep your expenses within that. There is enough for a very lavish treat." What he said was true, but the amount was wholly inadequate if I provided drinks, which they would expect.

We decided on a toddy shop near Changanacherry, where we

alighted at the bus stand and walked through a road with paddy fields on either side. The toddy shop was amidst a vast rice field connected to the road by a narrow walkway. Ducks swam along in the streams.

We sat on long wooden benches with desks and ordered a toddy pot for each.

"Food?" the waiter asked. "We have duck, chicken, prawns, frogs, mussels, crab, fish, and beef." A star hotel is unlikely to have such variety on the menu.

Each of us ordered a different dish so that we could try them all, with tapioca as the main dish. The evening passed quickly as we savored the fare and took large swigs from the toddy pots. Soon, many jugs were empty, and some ordered another urn.

I was already feeling tipsy and decided I'd had enough. Besides, I was worried about the bill. I had warned everyone that my total budget was hundred rupees, but Avaran had asked everyone not to restrict themselves. "This is a unique occasion, and we will enjoy it maximum."

Still, I felt apprehensive when orders were going out in rapid succession. "Another plate of prawns, please," then "one more duck" and later, "two pots of toddy!" I knew the bill would be way above a hundred. Avaran, who was sitting next to me, noticed my discomfiture. He leaned over and whispered in my ear. "Don't worry about the bill. I will pay whatever shortage you have." Reassured, I settled down to enjoy the party.

As time passed, the earthen pots of toddy kept coming, and all had become somewhat inebriated when Avaran announced. "It's getting dark. Time we made a move." Everyone got up one by one, taking considerable time and effort. They gathered outside while I waited with Avaran to pay the bill. It was 160 rupees. I handed over my hundred rupees and left him to settle the bill, which he did, adding a generous tip.

We started our long way back to the bus station. The colors of twilight lit up the sky, and we broke into a song as we strolled along. People passing us looked bemused; many gave an indulging smile, while others were not so amused.

I am not sure how the trouble erupted, but a brawl started with a group of people- seemingly laborers returning after work. It looked as if a fight was imminent. I made a quick assessment of the situation. We outnumbered them, but they were sturdy men armed with spades and sickles. It might be a bloody one if it came to an actual encounter. Will we all end up in jail with me missing the admission?

I knew I had to act fast to avert a confrontation. I tried to persuade Boban to back out, but he seemed adamant. The toddy in him had taken complete control, and I thought it might be better to try the sober guys. "Cheta," I pleaded. "Please excuse him. He just had a bit too much."

"If you consume toddy, it should stay in your stomach. Don't act smart with us locals here." He was unrelenting.

A sizable crowd had gathered by then, and they clearly outnumbered us. We are done for if these people are indeed from the local vicinity. Without hesitation, I fell at his feet, pleading. "Please forgive us. I hosted this party to celebrate my admission to medical college, but my friend got too drunk."

"So you are going to be a doctor? Better you keep clear of such friends." He gestured to the rest of his group. "Come, let's go. Ignore that guy." Boban was still in competitive form, challenging anyone for a duel, but the group just left, unmindful of his taunts. Boban never forgave me for my intervention, though I reminded him I might have saved his life that day.

35. A Medical Student!

The day arrived for my joining Medical College. The interview was in a large auditorium in the center of the college building, flanked on both sides by the various non-clinical departments and classrooms.

I noticed how everyone else had arrived with their parents, and it seemed I was the only one who had come alone. Going from table to table, with professors examining and verifying my certificates and mark sheets, I paid 700 rupees at the last table as the fees for the first year and confirmed my admission.

Opting for accommodation in the hostel, I paid seven rupees for a month's hostel rent to book my room. The clerk in charge of collecting the cash looked me up. Maybe noticing my extra-long frame, he remarked- "The hostel will not have many facilities. Seven or eight students might be in a room, and you will have to share a single table and bed." I wondered how eight people could share one bed.

Classes would start in two weeks. I had a white coat stitched by a local tailor, who did an elaborate job. Packing all my clothes and some books in two large suitcases, I stuffed snacks like banana chips, sweet rice balls, and other goodies my mother had made into a smaller bag.

I left home for the railway station in a taxi. This time, no one accompanied me to the station to bid goodbye, nor did my mother cry as I left home. I alighted at the small railway station nearest the medical college and took another taxi to the hostel.

As I was unloading my luggage on the front porch of the hostel, I could see many senior inmates watching me while lounging on a concrete bench on an unkempt lawn in front. One of them got up and approached me. "Sir, is anyone of yours joining the hostel?" he asked respectfully.

"I am joining," I answered while lifting the heavy suitcases from the taxi's boot.

"You! You son of a bitch! I felt deceived by your looks. You look old enough to be bringing your son to join. I called you 'Sir,' whereas you should call me that. As a punishment, call me 'Sir' a hundred times."

The taxi driver interrupted. "Pay my fare first," he demanded, amused at the situation. He took the money and sped away, not bothering to hide his glee.

"Sir, Sir, Sir, Sir, Sir…" I started my task. Many who had been lazing on the bench came forward and joined the ragging. "The nerve of this guy, joining hostel even before classes have started. People take at least a few days or weeks to be bold enough to step into this hostel!"

"Now, let's see what he has brought for us." Another guy was looking at my suitcases. "Open it!"

With trembling hands, I opened up the suitcases. "What is this? Your underwears are all the same color; the girls will think you have only one!" I kept quiet as he rummaged through all my clothes and came upon the packets of snacks my mother had packed.

"We are in luck!" screamed the guy as he fished out all the bundles. The crowd of seniors became bigger as everyone munched on the tidbits, praising my mother for her cooking skills and thoughtfulness. I thought they would offer me a small bite, but that was not to be. I watched as they gobbled the last morsel up.

"There seems to be nothing more for us here," he said as he closed the boxes. "Now, carry these suitcases to your room. After that, you will have your whole day cut out. It is unlikely that any other fresher will join the hostel today, so you are the only person available for entertainment for the three hundred odd seniors here. You can say goodbye to any thoughts of sleep tonight. We will all take turns at you."

I felt an impending doom as I picked up my luggage and followed him to my room. I recalled the words of MK- 'You might have to bear with some intense ragging when you join. Just go along and do what they say. Nobody has died or been grievously hurt by ragging in this hostel.'

I placed my belongings in my room and followed him upstairs as ordered. The senior escorting me up the stairs (Fernandez, as I was to learn later) was given initial rights to me as he had seen me first. He seemed to sense the dread in me, and a wave of sympathy flashed across his face as he turned to me.

"Ragging has to be gone through for any aspiring doctor, and it will make you tougher and equip you to face all future challenges that the world will offer."

I watched as his face changed again to become stern. "Now get going fast. We don't have all day! Once I get through you, there are so many others waiting."

I braced myself and hurried up behind him.

Epilogue

Twenty-five years later...

I am inside the Medical College auditorium. The atmosphere brings me a feeling of deja vu. Nothing much seems to have changed. There were the same rows of tables where professors checked the certificates and marks of the candidates selected for admission. The only significant change was a desktop computer on one table, where a clerk filled in the students' data.

We moved forward from table to table till we reached a senior madam. I recognized her as my former tutor in anatomy, then a good-looking, smart young lady. Age has withered her, but she still looked attractive and dignified, sitting at her table with poise.

She took the documents from my son and glanced through them. "Aju T Thomas," she read aloud, looked up at him, and then at me. Recognition dawned on her face, and she exclaimed. "Aren't you Thomas T Thomas? Is this your son?"

I nodded in confirmation. Madam put on a mischievous smile as she asked me. "Will he be as troublesome as you were?"

"No, Madam," I replied. "He is such a quiet and disciplined boy."

We had learned about his selection from the net and were thrilled to see his name pop up with a rank that was sure to get him a seat. We had no doubts as we opted for Trivandrum Medical College, my alma mater.

The system of admission had changed long back. Marks obtained in the qualifying course were irrelevant, and it was through a competitive test that successful candidates were chosen. Few made it in the first attempt, and the majority gained admission after intensive coaching for one year at any of the many coaching institutes which had sprung up all over the state.

Getting training from one of the esteemed centers was an expensive affair. Besides the tuition fees of above ten thousand rupees, the expenses for accommodation and food added up to a significant amount that made it inaccessible to students from poorer families.

Getting admission to a reputed coaching center was by itself a competitive affair. These institutes chose the best students based on their final school exam results. The number of students who got admission to professional colleges from their institute was crucial for them to advertise on the front pages of newspapers to attract the best students next year.

Aju had got admission on the second attempt. Soon after the final exam after 12th standard, he enrolled in a one-month crash course in a reputed center far off, in Trichur. The fee for just one month of coaching was twelve thousand rupees. We enrolled him there and put him as a paid guest in one of the many make-shift lodgings that mushroomed around the coaching center.

The coaching institute owned a hostel meant for the regular students of the one-year course. It was like a concentration camp. Rumors alleged they had hidden cameras everywhere to monitor the students, even over the beds in their dormitories. They had a strict timetable, with all the day's twenty-four hours scheduled out.

Not succeeding in the first attempt, we enrolled him in another coaching center for regular full-year coaching. It was an upcoming establishment nearer home. The coaching was equally intense, but they had a more humane approach. This time, Aju scored high in the entrance exam and could comfortably earn his medical seat.

Classes were to start after two weeks. We opted for accommodation in the hostel. Ragging was now strictly restricted, and the college employed two security guards to protect the first-years. They even banned the seniors from talking to the freshers.

Despite all these precautions, the seniors would find some way for a bit of ragging- on the way to college, inside the college bus, or while having food in the mess. I didn't worry much, as we had taught the children to be independent and self-reliant. Being a President Scout and a black belt in Karate, he should be able to fend for himself.

Formalities completed, we stepped out of the auditorium and found the spacious corridor in front overflowing with those waiting their turn. We had completed the process early because of my son's high rank on the list.

I noticed a person pushing himself towards us, with a boy, probably his son, tagging him. "TTT! Why are you here? Has any of your children got admission?"

I recognized Fernandez, the senior I first met in the hostel when I joined here as a medical student. He had changed a lot, and his hair had greyed. He looked tense. "Yes, Fernandez," I replied, pointing toward my son. "What about you?"

"My son has also got selected. He got selected with his first attempt and scraped through into the list, so he is at the bottom and will be called in late. It might be a long wait. Where have you taken accommodation for your son, TT? Is he joining the hostel?"

"Yes, of course! Why should we think of any other option?"

"I am worried about the ragging," Fernandez confided. "It seems it is stricter now, with special security for the freshers, but some guys somehow get hold of the first-years. I won't be able to sleep thinking about it. You see, he is my only son and has never been away from home."

Fernandez took out his kerchief and wiped the sweat off his brow.

I could see his hand trembling as he spoke. "But now I feel we will opt for the hostel. It's a great relief that your son will also be there."

"Yes," I said, turning to introduce Aju to his son, who emerged from behind his father, a small and timid figure. "But remember, my son is also a fresher."

I laid my hands on his shoulder and continued. "Don't lose sleep over it, Fernandez. Nobody here has ever been grievously hurt by ragging. It's not all that bad. A bit of ragging will be beneficial for him in the long run. It will make him tougher and equip him for future challenges as a doctor."

ABOUT THE AUTHOR

Dr. Thomas T. Thomas is a General Practitioner of varied experiences. He has worked in remote rural clinics, in various government Health centres, in casualty of major hospitals, and as visiting medical officer in plantations, industrial establishments and de-addiction centres. He is presently working full time as a Family Physician in Muthoot Medical Centre, Pathanamthitta.

He has multiple other interests like art, music, reading, cooking, computers, growing trees, and rearing fish. He describes himself as a Jack of all trades, though a master in none.

He now resides at his renovated ancestral house in his home village Mallassery, with his wife of more than thirty five years, Dr. Annie George, who looks after their own Family Clinic in the village. His son is an Orthopaedician married to an Ophthalmology student, and they have two children. His daughter is working as a Judicial Officer.

Website: http://www.drthomastthomas.com

OTHER BOOKS BY DR. THOMAS

Adventures of a Countryside Doctor : https://relinks.me/B08TMKH863

Adventures of a Medical Student : https://relinks.me/B0B9LF89R4

Ulnaattil Oru Doctor : https://relinks.me/B09NFNNCYY

(The award-winning Malayalam translation of 'Adventures of a Countryside Doctor' by Dr. I. Jayashree)